THE CURSE

Mandy Baker

Alice –

Dreams do come true!

Mandy Baker

1

To my husband- my rock, my best friend, my hero, and my inspiration

Acknowledgements

First, I would like to thank my husband for all of his support and for always believing in my dreams.

I would also like to thank my family who has always been there for me no matter what.

A big thank you goes to my sister who took the time out of her very busy schedule to edit for me.

Lastly, thank you to all of you who are reading this book, it means a lot to me to be able to share this with you all!

The Curse

Createspace Publishing

She whose mind is true

And whose heart is pure

Must be lost despite herself.

True love will find its strength within,

To be rejoined,

And break the curse for all eternity.

The Curse

Chapter 1

"Come on Alex. We have to go. This could be the find to make my career, and Babe; it could be exactly what you need to turn your reputation around. This could make people take you seriously...as they should."

Alex sighed and ran his hand through his hair in frustration. He didn't know why he bothered to argue with her. In all the time they had known each other, he had never won one. In fact, that was how they had met.

Liz and her team had travelled to an area near Egypt on a dig. They were making good progress, or so they thought. There was a problem they didn't know about yet. Alex had gotten to the artifact they were searching for first. He was a treasure hunter, and he was good at it. He had spent his entire adult life acquiring rare artifacts and selling them to the highest bidder. He could find anything the insanely rich were looking for to add to their collections. He didn't care what happened after he got paid; he got what he wanted and that was all that mattered.

He had swooped into the dig site, grabbed the artifact and gone back to his hotel room. In and out with no one being the wiser, or so he thought. That night right in the middle of a cold beer and bad TV, there was an incessant knocking at the door.

"Alright! Keep your pants on! I'm

coming!"

Alex raised his eyebrows as he opened

the door and saw the little spit fire of a woman

standing in front of him. She maybe came up to

his chest, her dark brown hair was pulled back

in a messy bun and she had curves in all the

right places. She was wearing short khaki

shorts, a well fitted brown tank top and hiking

boots. She had muscle tone that was easily seen

in both her arms and her legs. He swore there

was actually steam coming out of her ears as

she stood there with her hands on her hips,

tapping her foot rapidly.

"On second thought...I take that back. Maybe you don't have to keep your pants on." He grinned as her face, if it was possible, turned an even darker shade of red.

"Are you kidding me? Where is it? I want what you took from us! And I want it now! So, either get it for me, or get out of my way and I'll find it myself!"

Alex tried unsuccessfully to hide the surprise in his face. In all his years, he had never been caught before. How did she possibly know? He racked his brain trying to pinpoint something that had gone wrong, something he may have forgotten. Had someone seen him? Had he left one of his tools behind?

"I don't know what you are talking about. What could I possibly have that belongs to you? I don't even know you... Not that I'm opposed to changing that."

"That's bullshit and you know it. Get the artifact so I can get out of here and I never have to see you again."

He stood in the door way and shrugged his shoulders. She let out a growl deep down in her throat and tried to push past him into the room. At just over six feet and muscular, he stopped her easily at first. Then she punched him in the stomach and strolled past him. As he was trying to recover his breath she began searching through his things. He wasn't worried; no one had ever found the false back in his suitcase. He had smuggled many an artifact across boarders and not been caught yet. He really couldn't hide his shock and dismay when she walked right over to his suitcase, opened it up and pulled back the lining.

"Aha! I knew it was you! Jackass. Do you know what this is? It belongs in a museum, not in the hands of one of your low life buyers."

"Low life buyers? I'll have you know my clients are some of the richest people in the world."

"I don't care who they are. Stay away from my digs and stop selling priceless artifacts to the highest bidder or so help me, I will turn you in and ruin your life."

Alex was left standing there speechless. He wasn't sure how much time passed before he could even begin to try to figure out what had just happened. But, he was pretty sure he had just lost the biggest pay out of his career and he was pretty sure he was in love. She didn't know it then, but he was going to marry her one day.

Chapter 2

"Fine, Liz. You win. You always do anyway, isn't that how you got me to marry you? We can go to California. But, weren't you the one that insisted that this artifact was just a myth? You said it was a thing of legend and nothing more. So, why are you suddenly so insistent that we drop everything to rush out there on a long shot?"

"First of all, it was your sexy dark brown eyes and six pack abs that got me to marry you. And second, maybe, just maybe I was..." She swallowed hard. "Wrong."

"That must have hurt. I don't think I have ever heard you use those words before."

14

She playfully swatted at him and they laughed together.

"Seriously though, ever since I got wind of this new lead I've been doing some research. This might not be the myth people always thought it was. I really think there is something out there."

"Ok. I trust your instincts. But, answer me this…What is an ancient Egyptian artifact doing in an abandoned mining town in California?"

"I don't know. I think that is probably a question that can be answered once we get there."

Chapter 3

A few days later Alex found himself standing in the dusty sunshine and heat. He took his beat up old baseball cap. He'd had the hat for as long as he could remember, it was fitted and molded perfectly to his head; he'd always thought of it as a good luck charm of sorts. Alex had worn it on each of his jobs as a treasure hunter and had always found what he was looking for. Now, he wore it on digs. He wiped his brow and surveyed the small mining town. Everything was covered in dust, but the buildings all looked exactly like they had the last time the town was in use. It was almost as if everyone had simply disappeared. Newspapers lay long unread on dining room tables in the small cabins, the shelves of the General Store were still stocked with canned goods, and the mining carts were stopped in the middle of the tracks.

He was just beginning to unload their equipment and bags from the Jeep when he heard another vehicle coming up the dirt road. He turned around and saw four trucks and another Jeep driving up the road to where he was. He stood up and waited for them to stop.

"Can I help you guys?"

"Alex...You son of a bitch, we thought you were dead!"

"Not dead...Just married."

"Oh man! I can't believe it! Only you would beat us here."

"Well, Jim, you always were a little on the slow side."

"You always were a jackass."

They laughed and hugged it out. This is how Liz found them when she came out of one of the buildings. She stood there for a minute looking confused. She had never seen Alex act like this, and she definitely had never seen the man he was hugging. She stepped forward just as they started in on their "manly" banter again.

"Alex?"

"Oh, Honey! I was wondering where you got off to. This is Jim. He and I… Well, let's just say we go way back. He was always two steps behind me."

Alex playfully punched Jim's shoulder and laughed. Jim laughed too and then stepped toward Liz. She held out her hand to shake his and couldn't hold in a surprised yell when he picked her up in a bear hug.

"Put me down… Please put me down."

Her voice was stronger than she expected. She readjusted her clothing and smoothed it out after he put her down. Alex put his arm around her and grinned. She couldn't

help but smile despite herself; this was truly a
new side of her husband.

"Hey, Alex. You should know that we
may be the first, but we won't be the last. The
word is out on this. Everyone and their brother
are going to be showing up here looking for this
thing. It could get ugly."

"Yeah... I figured that as soon as I saw
your ugly face here. I guess we need to unload
and set up quickly so we can stake out our
area."

They had just finished setting up when
the rest of the people started arriving in turn.
Alex recognized many of them from the old
days. He was sure Liz recognized a few more

from her work. They all came in and set up their

areas. That first night they pretty much all kept

to their own groups.

Chapter 4

The next day the searching and digging began. It was no surprise that the archeologists and the treasure hunters butted heads, treasure hunters were never well known for tact and patience, and archeologists were renowned for their hard heads. But, it was when the treasure hunters brought out their explosives to explore a potential site that things really exploded. And leading the charge for the archeologist side was of course, Liz. She may be small, but she could stand her ground with the best of them.

Alex had learned long ago to let Liz fight her own battles, and busied himself a short

22

distance away. He couldn't fully hear what was being said, but he had a strange feeling that she was winning. She had a way of knowing just what a person's weakness was and being able to jab a dagger into it while not even breaking a sweat.

"FINE! DO IT YOUR WAY!"

Alex smiled to himself as the guy brushed passed him as he stormed off. He glanced up as Liz walked down the hill toward him, she had just the slightest hop to step and he could see the grin spreading across her face as she got closer. Alex stood and brushed his hands off.

"Pleased with yourself?"

Liz laughed as she walked into his embrace and leaned her head on his shoulder. He kissed the top of her head as he smiled. No one could make a man feel like he wanted to hit something and laugh at the same time like she could. He had seen it time and time again, and even experienced it himself once or twice. They were so angry that if she had been a man, they would have hit her. But, at the same time they had to keep themselves from laughing because of the little thing they were staring at that had just bested them.

Later that day Alex was sitting under one of the canopies cleaning tools when Jim came and sat next to him. Alex reached into a nearby container and handed him a water bottle. Jim took it gratefully and drank deeply. When he'd finished he looked at Alex.

"I know that look. What do you want?" Alex grabbed his own bottle and took a break from the tools in front of him.

"I have a proposal for you."

"I'm not sure I like the sound of that."

"Just hear me out. I got word on good authority about a... special item in a little town a few miles north of here. It would be a quick job, in and out. But, it has a big payday. I'll split it 50/50 with you. What do you say? It would be just like old times."

"Nah...I don't think so man."

25

"Come on. These guys don't know what they're doing. Not like you do. No one would even know we are gone. What's wrong haven't gone soft on me have you?"

"What the hell are you talkin' about?"

"I'm saying that since you got that fancy degree and a pretty wife you've gone soft. Your turning down the job of a lifetime because she has you so whipped you can't see straight anymore."

"You don't know anything, Asshole! Screw you! Get the hell out of here and I never want to see you again. I'm turning down your shitty job because my life with my wife is more important than any amount of money. It's taken

26

me a long time to figure this out, and it may surprise you, but there are more important things in life than money. Maybe one day you will figure that out for yourself...Now leave."

The last two words were no more than a growl as Alex turned his back and stocked off. Liz was around the corner and heard everything. Her eyes filled with tears, she was never prouder of her husband than right then. She knew how hard it was for him to turn his life around and equally hard it was for him to turn down a job like that. She wiped her eyes and went after him.

Chapter 5

Weeks went by without finding anything. Tensions grew to their boiling points and some gave up all together, packed up and went home. Everyone was wondering if maybe this artifact really was a myth and they have been on a wild goose chase this whole time. Everyone, that is, except Liz. Somehow she never lost her confidence. She knew they were going to find it and she wasn't leaving until they did.

Just as even Alex and the archeology team were beginning to doubt whether there was anything to be found, she did it. It was late afternoon, almost time to give up for the day.

She had been working in a cave overlooking the mining camp for a few days. Everyone had told her she was crazy for going up there; they were all convinced it had to be buried in the mine. However, no one had been able to prove that theory because there was an invisible force keeping them from entering the mine to explore it. That afternoon, the static of the walkie-talkie proved them all wrong.

"Alex. Alex are you there?"

"Yeah. Liz, what's up?"

"I found it! I found it! I found it!"

"What!? That's amazing! Ok, hang on. We'll be right up. Don't do anything until we get there."

Alex and the team grabbed their gear and headed up the hill to the cave. They were almost to the top when the ground began to shake. They looked for anything nearby to hold onto. Alex tried everything he could to keep his feet under him. All he could think of was getting to Liz. She was all alone in that cave and who knows what kind of damage an earthquake that strong could do.

But, he couldn't move. He couldn't even stay standing for more than a few seconds at a time. He was starting to panic. He had to get to her. What if there was a cave-in and she was trapped or hurt or worse. He had to get up the hill. He pushed himself up and used all the adrenaline in his body to force his legs to work and get him up there. After a few steps, just as

he was starting to fall again, the ground

stopped shaking. He caught himself and started

running.

"LIZ! Liz! Are you okay? Can you hear

me? Liz!? Answer me!"

He reached the top of the hill and the

entrance to the cave still calling her name.

There was no response. His heart started

beating faster. It felt as if it could pound out of

his chest. He didn't know what he would do if

he lost her. His life was nothing without her.

Just as he entered the cave there was a

great flash of light, and he was thrown

backwards. He felt his head hit the rocks and

31

then everything went black. When he woke up it was dark out. He slowly sat up as he rubbed his head. He dug his flashlight out of his backpack and looked around the cave. There was no sign of a dig...and no sign of Liz.

He stepped outside and looked around. It was so dark he had a hard time seeing even with his flashlight, but from his vantage point, there were no signs of anyone. He ran down the hill to where their camp should've been. But, it was gone. The tents, the equipment, even the vehicles were all gone. They had simply disappeared. And there was no one in sight. He didn't understand what had happened. What could've made everything just disappear? And where was everybody? Where was Liz?

Chapter 6

Alex sat back and pulled off his reading glasses. He sighed and pinched the bridge of his nose. His dark brown hair that he usually kept short had grown longer and was a little bit shaggy. His hard, square jaw had a little bit more than a five o'clock shadow on it. As he set his glasses onto the table in front of him, he looked around. He was the only one down there; it was after all the basement archives of a prestigious university. Not just anyone was granted access. On a normal day he wouldn't have been either. But, they all knew his wife and they knew the research that had taken him all over the world for the past seven months. *Seven months...* Had it really been that long

since everything had gone so horribly wrong in
California? So many people had simply vanished
and Alex still had no idea how or why he had
escaped.

Now seven months later, he was in yet
another dingy library desperately digging for
clues. Trying to find any hint as to what had
happened and where Liz was. She wasn't dead.
He could feel it.

"But where are you, Liz? What am I
supposed to do?" His questions echoed back at
him as he sat there twisting his wedding band
around his finger, as he often did when he was
thinking of her.

His fervent search had begun about three days after he returned to their cabin in the mountains of Vermont. He barely remembered the flight back from California. His head was still foggy and he couldn't wrap his mind around the fact that everyone, especially Liz, was simply gone. He figured no one would believe him if he told them. He also knew he had to do something, but he had no idea what. He spent the entire car ride up the mountain deep in thought. He had forced himself to hold it together on the long plane ride, as he felt the air cool and he smelt the deep scent of the maple and oak trees through the open window he knew he was almost there. Just a few more miles and he would be at the cabin. They lived in New York City most of the time. It was the

best place to be for Liz's work with the

museums. But, they both loved the outdoors

and craved a place to get away from the city

and to relax after long digs. So, they had

travelled deep into the mountains of Vermont

until they had found the perfect piece of land.

It had taken them over a year, but each

layer of that cabin had been lovingly laid with

their own hands. The only time they called in

the experts was for the electricity and the

plumbing. Otherwise they chose to do it

themselves; just the two of them lost in the

woods building their dream get away home. As

he pulled up to the front of the cabin, he saw

the cheerful flowers lining the beds in front of

the wrap around porch. Liz had no idea what they were called, but she had loved their colorful patterns and had put them in with no real plan. But, somehow it had worked. He saw their two rocking chairs sitting on the porch waiting for them to sit in them with their morning coffee or watch the sunsets with a cold beer on a hot summer night.

He felt the emotions begin to bubble up inside of him and he quickly made his way up the front steps and through the door. It was when he stepped inside and closed the door that he lost the last pretext of control he had held. Every inch of that cabin screamed of Liz. She had picked each piece of furniture and decorated herself. It even smelled like her

37

favorite spice scented candles, even though

they hadn't been burned in months. He slid

down the door until he felt himself hit the floor.

Alex dropped his head into his hands and wept.

Chapter 7

Alex slept for nearly two days. When he finally pulled himself out of bed he felt worse than when he had crawled into it. He stumbled into the bathroom, cranked the shower to its hottest setting and stepped inside. Alex let the hot water cascade over his body as he leaned his head against the shower wall. The thought was like a slap to his face when it came to him.

What are you doing? Feeling sorry for yourself? Get your ass out there and find your wife! You are the only one who can!

He wasn't sure where the voice came from, but it was just the kick in the butt he needed. Alex finished his shower and dressed

39

quickly. He turned on the coffee pot as he pulled his t-shirt over his still wet hair. Then he walked over to the computer and powered it on. He wasn't sure where to start, but he figured searching online was as good place as any.

Twelve hours and four pots of coffee later, Alex was more than frustrated. He had exhausted every source he could think of online. He felt like he had taken one step forward and ten steps backwards. He had no idea how it was possible to do that much online research and come up empty handed. How deep did this thing go? How far back? Alex knew that this was way over his head and there was no way he was going to find answers on his own. It was time to call in reinforcements.

He dialed the number for Liz's boss at the museum. While he waited on hold he thought about the reaction Bob would have. He must have heard about what had happened by now. Everyone was probably talking about it. He tried to prepare himself for Bob's typical over the top reaction. But, when Bob finally answered in his familiar British accent, overreaction wasn't what Alex heard in his voice.

"Alex! How goes the dig? I'm surprised to hear from you way over there in the California desert!"

41

"Hey Bob...." Alex trailed off. He was confused. He would have thought that word had travelled by now. But, then it hit him. They weren't due for check-ins for another week, and he was the only one left. In the days since he made it home, the phone hadn't rang once. Of course Bob didn't know about Liz! Alex took a deep breath and sighed, now he had to be the one to break the news...This was going to be interesting.

"Bob....Bob hang on a second, can you stop for a second? There is something I need to tell you." While Alex was putting his thoughts together, Bob had been rattling on in his usual manner about who knows what.

"Something happened on the dig, something bad. I'm not even really sure how to tell you this."

"Well, bloody hell, Alex what is it? Spit it out! Has something happened to Liz?"

Alex sighed again. He could picture Bob sitting in his cluttered office, behind his gorgeous antique mahogany desk which was always buried under a mountain of papers, folders and books. He would be vigorously chewing gum, wishing they hadn't changed the smoking laws. Back in the day, Bob was never without his cigar. Now, since he could no longer smoke in the building he coped in different ways. Bob was old school; he was in his early fifties but was still in incredible shape. His hair

was the same color brown it had been when he

was twenty. He was tall and slender; not an

ounce of fat on his whole body. His skin was

surprisingly light for the fact that he spent most

of his life out in the sun on digs. He had a

crooked smile that made you think he knew

something you didn't; and usually he did.

" Bob...Something has happened to Liz.

And I'm going to need your help."

Chapter 8

The next morning Alex found himself on a plane. He was heading to what would turn out to be the first of many prestigious universities. He spent the next seven months going through every old and dusty manuscript or book that mentioned the artifact. He must have been in every dank and musty basement in both Europe and the United States.

Now sitting in that final dusty basement, Alex's frustration level rose. He had to figure out what he was doing wrong. The answer had to be out there somewhere. Then it hit him. He got so excited that he knocked his chair over when he stood up. He had spent this

45

whole time focusing on the artifact. But, what if the answer didn't lie with that but with the mine or the town?

He kicked himself for not thinking of it sooner, he had lost so much time focusing on the artifact. There it was, in the first book he looked at. During the height of the California Gold Rush the town had been booming. Someone on was striking gold nearly every week. The mine expanded farther and farther into the mountain and each miner had nothing but fortune on their minds. One fateful day, a group of them decided they needed to break away from the mine and the large number of miners in it and strike out on their own. They knew they shouldn't stray too far because there was still wealth to be found in the area. So, they

began to hike up the hillside that overlooked

the town. They didn't have to hike too far

before they stumbled across a strange cave

gaping open on the side of the hill. Excitedly

they lit their lanterns and crept inside. The men

set up a small camp just inside the cave

entrance and immediately began carving into

walls, hoping get lucky and strike it rich. After

only a few days of digging, one of them struck

gold, and their fates were sealed.

The late afternoon sun hung high in the

blue desert sky, baking the ground below and

forcing the temperature to rise inside the cave.

The men wiped the sweat out of their eyes and

did a double take on the shining gold object

47

peeking out from the dark stone wall of the

cave. None of them could quite place what they

were looking at, but they knew it was out of

place in the California desert. They glanced at

each other and shrugged. It didn't matter to any

of them what it was or where it was from; it

was solid gold. Their whoops and hollers

echoed out of the cave and down the hillside.

They had struck gold and they were going be

rich. The men worked to dig the artifact out of

the wall, and they almost got as lucky as they

thought themselves to be.

That was where the trail ran cold. Alex

furiously flipped through the book he was

reading out of and found nothing more on that

day. He slammed the book shut and quickly

went over to the shelf where he'd found it. There had to be other books there that discussed the town. He flipped through an entire shelves worth of books as quickly as he could. When he finally found another mention of the town, an entire year had been lost. No one knows what happened that day. A new group of miners hungry for gold made their way into the town. They had all heard the stories of how lucky the mine here was and they couldn't wait for their chance inside. But, when they arrived they couldn't believe what they had found. The town was quiet, there was no one working the mine and the buildings were empty.

The miners went from building to
building furiously trying to find any sign of
people. The general store still had stocked
shelves and many of the houses had
newspapers laid out on the tables. The date on
the newspapers was from a year before. They
left the town as quickly as they could and never
looked back. There was no sign of what had
happened to the people in the town a year ago,
but they were weren't sure they wanted to
know. Their stories became those that were
told on drunken nights and laughed about. No
one believed them and when they mentioned
the idea that some sort of curse had come over
that town, they were laughed out of every
saloon they stepped into. The town was left to

fall into ruins. The only problem was, despite the desert heat and storms, the town still stood exactly the way it had been more than a hundred years ago.

"A curse?" Alex furrowed his brow, totally unaware he was talking to himself out loud. "That's not possible. Curses aren't real!"

He flipped through a couple more books and found nothing else mentioning the town or the people who had disappeared. Even so, he had still found something. Alex began to get even more excited. It may not have been much, but he finally gotten a break. He was still having trouble with the idea of a curse, but at

51

least now he knew there were similar instances

before this. He stopped for a moment. *Could*

this be connected to Roanoke also? He shook his

head to clear it, he had to stay focused and he

needed to call Bob! He pulled out his cell

phone, only to find that he had no service in the

basement. He wasn't sure his feet even touched

the ground as he ran up the steps.

He stepped out into the bright New

England sunshine and breathed in the fresh air.

As he dialed Bob's number, his mind wandered

to the day about six months after Liz had burst

into his room in Egypt and took back the

artifact. In those six months, he hadn't been

able to get her out of his mind. She intrigued

him in ways that no woman had ever been able

to do. He loved her feistiness and that she wasn't intimidated by him. The fact that she called him on his shit made him smile every time he thought about it.

He was in Montana scoping out a new find for a client. He was secretly hoping that her team might be there. He was beginning to feel disappointed though. He'd been here for a week trying to find the exact location of this elusive piece. He was surprised that there wasn't an archeological team here at all. He figured they would have been all over this. He was in an open field outside of the town scoping it out as a possible location for the piece he was looking for; he was just about to move on when he heard a familiar voice coming from behind him.

"What the hell are you doing here?"

Alex smiled to himself before he turned around with a stern look on his face. He had waited six months for this moment and he was going to milk it.

"What do you mean what the hell am I doing here? I'm doing my job."

"Job? I am not sure what you do can be considered a real job."

Alex pretended to take offense to that. But, the truth was he had grown tired of the treasure hunting and dealing with the rich asshole clients who felt they were entitled to whatever they wanted simply because they had money. He had been thinking of getting out of the game for a while. He couldn't let her know that though.

"So...Are you going to answer my question? What the hell are you doing here? This is our dig and you are not getting your hands on this one."

"Your dig? I've been here for a week already. It's not my fault you and your team were slow on the up take."

She growled and turned to walk away. Alex quickly reached out and grabbed her arm. The look on her face told him that may not have been the best idea. But, he couldn't let her get

away again.

"Have dinner with me."

"Why would I do that?"

"Because as much as you pretend to

dislike me, you secretly find me adorable."

She stared at him for a moment. He

watched the battle going on in her head

through her eyes. He could tell that she really

didn't want to admit that she was as intrigued

by him as he was by her. Finally, she gave half a

smile and nodded her head.

"Meet me at the diner at seven."

Chapter 9

"Bob, I found her. At least, I am pretty sure I've figured things out." Alex relayed the story of the miners and the people in the town to Bob.

"It's the craziest thing, Bob. Everything just drops off on that day when those miners found the artifact. Then a year later, people were writing about how it was as if everyone had disappeared into thin air."

"Bollocks…" Alex waited for Bob to continue. "That's got to be what happened to Liz! So, what do we do now?"

Alex hadn't figured that part out yet. That question made him feel once again like he had taken one step forward and about ten steps

backwards. In many ways, he was right back at

square one. Sure, he may have discovered the

curse. But, he was in new territory. He had

never come face to face with a curse before. In

fact seven months ago, he would have told you

there was no such thing as curses. If he hadn't

seen it with his own eyes, he still would have

thought it was total bullshit. He ran his hands

through his hair.

"Damned if I know, Bob. Hell, I am still

trying to wrap my head around the fact that this

is really happening. I've travelled to the most

remote places on Earth and I have unburied

artifacts that you would drool over. But, not

once did I ever find a damn thing that would

make me say that curses are real. I mean, a few months ago I would have told anyone who tried to tell me differently that they were crazy."

Crazy is exactly how Alex had felt on his first date with Liz. He couldn't remember a time when a woman had made him feel so undone. From the time he had hit puberty he had been nothing but confident with women. His first girlfriend had been the head cheerleader at his Jr. High school and he had dated only the most popular girls while he was in High School. As he got older he had never been in want for the company of a beautiful woman. But, Liz was different. He felt so awkward and unlike himself around her. She made him feel uncomfortable and out of control in the most amazing way.

The night of their first date, he was so nervous that he changed his shirt four times and arrived at the diner an hour early. He was afraid she wasn't going to show up. He sat at the counter and ordered a beer to help calm his nerves. As he sipped it, he reminded himself to take it easy and ran his hand through his hair. It was as dark brown and he always kept it short, to make it easier for his lifestyle. There were times he was in places that he never knew where his next shower was coming from. He fidgeted, and adjusted his grey button down shirt. He knew the dark charcoal brought out his brown eyes and that the dark wash jeans he paired with it fit him well, but he was worried what she would think of his outfit.

He was just finishing his beer when she walked in the door. He nearly choked on his last sip when he saw her, she was standing at the front door scanning the room, looking for him. She was wearing an ivory maxi dress and dark brown sandals. Her brown hair was pulled back in that familiar messy bun and her skin glistened with a new tan from hours of working in the hot sun. He set his empty bottle on the counter and walked toward her.

"Hey." The word was barely audible as he let out the breath he had been holding.

"Hey, yourself." She smirked and let him lead her toward the waitress waiting to seat them.

The Curse

The restaurant was a typical small town diner, booths lined the windows and there were a few tables scattered here and there across the floor. On the other side of a lattice divider that was covered in silk flowers and ivy a bar counter ran from one side to the other, giving an almost unobstructed view of the cooks in the kitchen. At one end of the counter sat homemade pies under glass domes. The smell of greasy food wafted through the air. The waitresses all wore Wranglers and a different colored plaid button down shirt. It wasn't a five star restaurant, but it was the best they could do in the Middle- of –Nowhere, Montana.

Their waitress was wearing a bright pink short sleeved plaid shirt with pearly buttons running down her expansive bosom, pulling at their seams and boot cut jeans that made one wonder how she fit them over her bottom that matched the bosom, seated them in a back corner booth. The table was a little bit sticky and the benches were covered in red vinyl that looked as if it had been there since the diner opened fifty years ago. The menu had the usual fare from breakfast served all day to a meatloaf special. The first few minutes after they had ordered were spent in an uncomfortable silence with Liz staring at him with contempt.

"If you are going to sit there and judge me all night, why did you agree to come?"

The Curse

He watched her with curious eyes as she sipped her beer; he tried to figure her out but couldn't get a read on her. She hadn't said more than two words to him since she arrived. She had agreed to have dinner with him, but she didn't seem to want to talk or even be there with him. He couldn't figure out why she had agreed to come in the first place.

"I'm here to keep my eye on you. If you are here with me, you can't go and raid our dig."

"Excuse me. I happen to be very good at what I do. I've done the leg work and I have no need to raid your dig as you say. I could go out there tomorrow and get what I need without any help from you people." He knew what he was saying was a lie, he had no idea where to find the piece, but she was being so judgmental he had to make her think he hadn't simply spent a week in the middle of Montana waiting for her.

She snorted in disbelief. Alex had no idea how one person could be so frustrating yet so intriguing at the same time. There was a part of him that wanted to strangle her or at least to get up and walk out of that diner and never see her again. But, he couldn't seem to make his legs work. He was glued to that vinyl bench.

Their food arrived and they began to eat in silence. The conversation may have been

65

lacking, but at least the food was good. He watched in wonder as she ate her cheeseburger; most of the women he dated refused to eat more than a salad on a date. But, she attacked her burger with zeal. She asked the waitress for another beer and raised her eyebrows at him in question, he nodded and she held up two fingers to double the order as the waitress walked away. He took that as his opening.

"So, what made you want to be an archeologist?"

She seemed to completely ignore is question, Alex sighed in frustration. She continued to eat her dinner in silence. But, now she was studying him and he noticed that the contempt was fading from her eyes even just a little bit. He wasn't sure what it was being replaced with, but he took it as a good sign. She pushed her plate away, and leaned back, staring at him as she sipped the last of her beer.

"If you are so good and don't need 'us people' to find what you need, then why have you been here so long. Shouldn't you have gotten what you need and been on your way by now? What are you still doing here?" Alex knew he was busted.

"Well, if you must know. I was hoping to run into you. I thought some verbal abuse would be a fun way to end my week."

Her bottle paused in midair and he was

afraid he had lost her for good. Then she

started laughing. He was surprised at first and

then couldn't help joining in. She had the most

infectious laugh and when she snorted, he

laughed harder than he had in a very long time.

When they were finally able to contain

themselves, she had tears running down her

face. After that the conversation seemed to

flow naturally.

Chapter 10

Alex was walking down a long dark corridor. He wasn't sure where he was, but the smell of damp dirt lingered in the air and burned the inside of his nostrils when he inhaled. He blindly felt around for something to indicate where we he was and found nothing. He stopped walking, and listened for a minute. In the distance he heard someone yelling. The voice sounded familiar. Was that Liz?

He began to run, calling her name. "Liz! Liz, is that you?! Where are you Baby?!"

As he turned a corner, he saw something out of the corner of his eye. He turned to look and there was nothing there, but he had the feeling he was being followed. It was

gaining on him. He tried to run faster. It seemed

the faster her ran, the more it gained on him.

He could feel a warm breath on his neck and all

the hairs stood up on end. He turned to look

again and still saw nothing behind him. He

pushed himself and ran even faster. He felt

fingers graze his shoulder and he screamed.

Alex sat up in bed drenched in sweat

and still screaming. He looked around and

wiped his face. It took him a minute to

remember that he was back at the cabin. He

had come back to regroup and to figure out his

next move. He threw back the covers and

stumbled into the bathroom. He stood at the

sink for a moment trying to catch his breath. He

70

splashed some cold water on his face and tried

to wash the dream away.

When that didn't work he pulled his

pants on and walked into the kitchen. He put

some ice into a glass and poured some whiskey

over the top. As he took a slow drink, he looked

out the window into the moonless night. The

darkness and seclusion of the woods

surrounding the cabin had never bothered him;

in fact that was part of what had drawn him and

Liz to that location in the first place. That night,

however, he wished he was in their apartment

in the city instead. He would have welcomed

the lights and the noise at that moment.

He knew he wasn't going to be able to go back to sleep, so he turned on the coffee pot and booted up his computer. He had to figure out where to go from here. He couldn't just sit around and do nothing. He knew that Liz was out there somewhere. She wasn't dead, he could feel it. But, where was she and how did he find her? Those were the questions that Alex was struggling to answer. He knew that he would probably need to head back to California. However, he didn't want to rush out there unprepared. Whatever this curse was that took Liz and the others, was ancient and he had to know what he was facing.

He had been all over the world researching for seven months. He felt no closer to finding the truth than the day he got back from California. Bob had tried to help as much as he could, but even he was out of resources. The artifact seemed to be secondary to the curse; it seemed to be more of a trigger than the actual cause. From what Alex and Bob had found, the artifact lured people in with their greed. When they discovered it, they and anyone nearby were then taken. They were still working on the where part of the whole situation, but it was looking like this curse was not picky about who ended up sucked into it.

What would Liz do? Alex thought as he raked his hands through his hair and across the stubble on his face. *She always seems to know exactly what to do and what the answers are.*

73

But how does she do it? How does she always just know?

He had always known there was something different about her. From the day she had stormed into his hotel room in Egypt, he had known that she wasn't like other women. He didn't just mean she was different because of her personality; she was really different. First of all, she had known he had taken something from the dig site and he *knew* he hadn't been seen. Second, she had known where the secret compartment in his suitcase was; she had walked right over to it. He had passed through customs hundreds of times and no one had found that compartment. It was even lined so that x-ray machines couldn't see

74

inside it. But, she had simply known it was there.

Alex began twisting his ring around his finger. She had always mystified him. Even now years later, he still hadn't quite figured her out. He had brought it up before and asked her how she knew things that she shouldn't know. But, she had simply smiled at him and then either distracted him with her kisses, changed the subject or lashed out at him. Eventually Alex decided it wasn't important to him and let it drop.

He was pulled from his thoughts by a knock at the door. He jumped and his heart started beating faster. *Who could that be at this time?* Alex stood up from his chair and slowly walked towards the door, he pulled back the edge of the curtain and peered out the window just next it. He broke out into a grin when he saw who was standing there. He opened the door and pulled the man into a hug.

"Bob, you son of a bitch, what are you doing here?"

"I couldn't just sit there and do nothing, you wanker. So, I decided to come out and see if I could help you; drove all night to do it too. Don't thank me or anything."

"It's good to see you man. Come in."

"Is that coffee I smell?"

Alex nodded and headed off to the kitchen as Bob brought his bag in and set it down. He looked around the cabin and felt the sadness overwhelm him. He could feel Liz in every corner.

"Are you sure you wouldn't prefer tea?" Alex called from the kitchen.

"You know I can't stand that bloody stuff."

"I thought all you Brits turned your noses up at coffee because tea was a superior drink." Alex said laughing as he carried in two steaming mugs full of black coffee. It was a familiar banter; he had always teased Bob over the fact that he must be the only British person alive that hated tea that much. Alex motioned toward the couches in the living room and he handed Bob one of the steaming mugs as they sat.

Bob took a careful sip of the hot coffee and sighed with contentment. He leaned back and studied Alex. Bob was worried about him. Alex was lost in thought once again twisting his wedding ring around his finger; Bob knew he was thinking about Liz. Ever since their wedding day, when they had been separated Alex was usually messing with that ring in one way or another; it was automatic every time she crossed his mind.

"Are you ok, Alex?"

"I'm fine." He said as he nodded, dark clouds moving across his eyes.

Bob just looked at him. "What, I'm fine. Stop giving me that look, it creeps me out and just pisses me off."

"Well, I'll stop looking at you like this when you admit you might not be as fine as you say. You look like hell."

Alex sighed and took a long drink of his coffee. He knew that Bob wouldn't let up until he spilled his guts and at this point he could use the help. So, he gave in and told Bob everything. He told him about his frustration with the research, his worries, and even the dream that still had him shaken. When he had finished, he waited for Bob's reaction. When he didn't give one right away Alex let out an annoyed sigh and raked his hand through his hair.

"If you stay this wound up, you'll be bald before we know it." That made Alex laugh a little as he took a sip of his coffee.

Chapter 11

That night Alex found himself back in the dark tunnel. The same damp dirt smell lingered inside his nostrils. This time though, it was light enough that he could somewhat make out the area around him. He turned and saw the hint of a light coming from somewhere down the way. It was then that he heard it again, Liz's voice calling out his name.

He started running toward the light. He had that feeling again; a strange presence was behind him. It was gaining on him. Alex pushed himself to run faster. But, it seemed no matter how fast he ran it just got closer and closer. He felt its warm breath on the back of his neck, and the hairs stood on end. Just as he thought he had reached the end of the tunnel where the light was shining, he felt the same mysterious hand on his shoulder.

Alex woke up to his own screams and Bob shaking him awake. He sat up in his bed and ran his hand down his face. It came off wet with sweat. He knew Bob was talking to him and asking him something, but he couldn't make his mind focus on it. It was like his head was in a tunnel and he could just hear the echo of Bob's voice. He swung is legs over the side of the bed and sat there with his head down for a moment. He jumped when he felt Bob's hand on his shoulder.

"Alex...Alex, can you hear me?"

"Yeah..Yeah, I'm ok."

"Yeah, you look ok. Bloody hell, I've never been so scared in my life."

Alex nodded as he stood up. As he did, Bob sank down and sat on the edge of his bed. In a replay of the day before, Alex went into the bathroom and splashed cold water on his face. He had to figure out what these dreams meant, or they were going to be the death of him. He didn't know how much longer he could survive on so little sleep. And now he was keeping Bob up as well, and Lord knows what Bob is like when he doesn't get his beauty sleep.

He looked at himself in the mirror, Bob was right, he looked like hell. Alex sighed, ran his hands through his hair and turned to walk back into the bedroom. Bob was still sitting on the edge of the bed with his head in his hands. Alex walked over and put his hand on his shoulder and gave it a little squeeze. Bob looked up at him and gave him half a smile.

"I'm alright now, Bob. Go back to bed. One of us should get some sleep."

"No really, I'm ok. I'm here for you, whatever you need…"

Alex shook his head, interrupting Bob's sentence. He patted Bob on the back and sent him to his room to try to get some sleep. Alex

84

knew he wasn't going to be able to sleep. He

pulled a t-shirt on over his head as he walked

down the hall. He went into the kitchen and

turned on the coffee pot. He slammed his fist

against the counter. This was all becoming too

familiar and he was tired of it. Hell, he was tired

in general. He filled a mug with coffee and

walked into the study. He stood at the door way

for a minute, the memories filling his mind.

He saw Liz sitting behind the desk with

papers spread everywhere and her hair in a

messy bun on the top of her head. She was

researching a project and was lost in the work.

She was looking for something underneath the

papers in front of her and then on top. He

laughed to himself as he walked in the room

and pulled her pencil out from her hair and handed it to her. It was a familiar routine and she smiled at him as she took it.

He turned to the overstuffed, leather chair in the corner. Alex saw her sitting there with her legs flung over one arm. She had a well-worn book across her lap and a steaming cup of coffee in one hand. Her reading glasses were sliding down her nose and she scrunched it up to readjust them. She had always done that. He was never sure if it was because her hands were usually full or just a habit. But, it was one of the quirks that made him love her even more.

"Damn it, Liz. What am I supposed to do now? I'm so lost without you…"

He walked over to the chair and sank down into it. He had gone his whole life not depending on or trusting anyone but himself. His parents had died in a car crash when he was little and his aunt who raised him was an alcoholic who could've cared less what he did. When he was sixteen, he decided he couldn't handle it anymore and he left. He never heard from his aunt again and he wasn't even sure she had really realized that he was gone. As far as he knew, she had never tried to find him or anything. He had taken off and headed straight for the Florida coast.

He had no idea what he was going to do when he got there. All he knew is that he wanted to escape the Midwest winter and live in the sunshine. He figured that a good looking guy like himself wouldn't have too hard of a time finding work down there. Somehow as he was hitch hiking down to Florida, he ended up passing straight through the state and down into the Keys.

It didn't take him long to find a job on the docks with a fishing boat. After a couple of months working there, he saw a different kind of boat pull into the harbor. He had never seen a boat like that before. It was bigger than most of the fishing boats, and had strange equipment

on the back. As they tied up to the dock, Alex
walked over to the boat.

"Can I help you, pal?"

"What kind of boat is this?"

"We're treasure hunters."

The next day Alex left his position on
the fishing boat to take one up on the treasure
hunting boat. The captain accepted him right
away and took Alex under his wing. Alex stayed
on board for about four years. It was then that
Alex felt like he had to strike out on his own. He
had learned everything he could at sea with
those men and had become complacent. He
needed something more.

With the captain's blessing, he left the boat when they pulled back into port. He'd already gained a reputation through the crew, so it wasn't hard for him to begin building contacts of his own. He began to travel all over the world, finding artifacts and treasures for rich collectors. His methods were controversial, but they got the job done. He quickly became the guy everybody wanted. He was never in one place for more than a week. He travelled so much that he didn't feel the need to have a home base; he lived in hotels and out of his suitcase.

The day he met Liz, when she burst into his room and his life, was the day after he turned thirty. He'd been treasure hunting for ten years at that point and felt like he was on

top of the world. He was the best at what he

did. He had more money than he could spend in

a lifetime. And he had pretty girls in his bed

whenever he wanted, but was never tied down;

most of the time he chose to be alone. He

preferred to be by himself, and he liked not

having to answer to anyone. There was a part of

him that felt like ten years was a long time to

live out of a suitcase and never stop moving. He

thought maybe it was time for him to get out of

the game and settle down. Until Liz came

suddenly into his life though, he didn't really

have a reason to do it.

After their first date in Montana, he

realized that he was tired of the life he was

living. He hated looking over his shoulder all the time and he was also tired of being seen as and feeling like a low life. That night, after their first date, he decided he was done. He wouldn't be taking any more jobs and he was going to change his life. That's exactly what he did. He left Montana and bought a house on the East Coast, somewhat close to the museum Liz worked at. He got his GED and applied to college. He figured he would get his degree and become legit. Instead of being a controversial treasure hunter, he would be become an archeologist. That way he could still travel and do what he loved, but it would be in a way both he and Liz could be proud of.

Chapter 12

Liz was the first person he had ever

trusted and truly opened himself up to. Alex

had let himself come to depend on her. Now

that she was gone he had no idea how to live

without her and it pissed him off. He had

depended only on himself for his whole life, and

then Liz comes along, works her way behind his

walls, and then up and disappears.

How dare she? She manipulates me into

going to California with her. Then she insists on

going up to that damned cave by herself. She

knows how much I need her and still, all she

could think about was the dig and the next big

find! Did she ever once stop to think about me...about us? Noooo....

Lost in his thoughts and anger, Alex never heard Bob come into the study. Darkness had clouded his eyes and Bob furrowed his brow in concern. He had never seen Alex look this way and he wasn't sure what to do or say. Bob started to walk over to him, but something in the way Alex was sitting and the way he looked at him, made Bob hesitate.

Fueled by lack of sleep, nightmares, and adrenaline from his frustration Alex looked around for an outlet. Bob was standing there and he was as good as anything else. So, Alex rose from the chair with his fists clenched tight.

He wasn't sure why he did it, but he took a swing at Bob simply because he was there and he wasn't Liz. Bob ducked Alex's attack and quickly moved behind him and grabbed his arm. He twisted it up and held it against Alex's back. The more Alex struggled, the tighter Bob's grip became.

"What the hell are you even doing here, Bob?!" Alex shouted, still struggling to free himself.

"What the bloody hell am I doing here?!" Bob shouted back as he released Alex with a shove, causing him to fall back into the chair. "I'm bloody here to help you find your bloody wife and one of my oldest friends! You

The Curse

can bloody well push me away and pick a fight if you want. But, one, I would bloody kick your bloody ass and two, I'm not bloody going anywhere!"

Alex watched Bob storm out and dropped his head into his hands. He didn't know what was wrong with him. He wasn't himself. He was so frustrated with not being able to do anything to find Liz. But, he knew that Bob didn't deserve to be his punching bag, figuratively or literally.

He had to do something. He didn't know what, yet. He had to figure it out quick before he lost what was left of his sanity and did something really stupid. First though, he

96

needed to apologize to Bob and take a shower, not necessarily in that order.

After a long hot shower, Alex felt a little bit better and ready to face Bob again. He found him in the guest room packing his bag. Alex felt the anger building inside him again, but forced it down. He clenched his jaw and walked into the room. He saw some old books lying around open to different pages. But, otherwise the room was pristine and most of Bob's stuff was already hidden away in his well-worn leather bag.

"Bob? I thought you weren't going anywhere..." Alex said quietly, trailing off as he looked around.

"Alex, don't be such a wanker. *I'm* not going anywhere....*We* are going to California." He glanced up and saw the confused look on Alex's face. Bob sighed. "It is time for you to stop sulking. Sitting here and festering in your own anger is not going to bring Liz back. I'm still not sure what will, but I know we aren't going to find the answers here. We are going to go to California and we are going to tear that bloody ghost town apart until we find her. "Alex nodded and put his hand on Bob's shoulder before heading to his room to pack his own bag.

Chapter 13

Alex spent the flight deep in thought. He was so anxious he couldn't sleep; he couldn't even concentrate on his book or any of the magazines in the pocket of the seat in front of him. All he wanted to do was land so they could find Liz.

He glanced over at Bob who was sound asleep in the seat next to him. Alex shook his head, he had no idea how he could sleep at time like this. Finally, the announcement came over the loud speaker for the passengers to prepare for landing. Bob lifted his head, stretched and glanced out the window. Alex's heart began to beat faster as he felt the landing gear descend. He thought for sure it would beat right out of his chest when the tires made contact with the runway.

After battling the people at baggage claim and then at the car rental company Alex and Bob were finally on the road. They had a good four hour drive ahead of them and Alex was anxious to get going. Since Bob was so well rested from the flight, Alex made him drive. He sat in the passenger seat of the Jeep and watched the city fade away. It didn't take long for them to hit open road. Bob leaned back, set the cruise control and turned up the radio.

Alex looked over at his friend. He knew he could have done this himself; he had been a loner his whole life. But, he found himself

thinking he was really glad Bob was there with

him. It was funny, usually Bob was the one that

was full of nerves, this time it was Alex. He felt

the knot in his stomach tighten and turn; like

there was a hot rock sitting in his gut. Ever since

they had left his cabin in the woods of Vermont,

he had a feeling of dread come over him. It was

almost as if there was a black cloud hanging

over their every move.

He leaned back in his seat and closed

his eyes. He was hoping that maybe his mind

would be quiet long enough for him to get some

sleep. He hadn't really slept in three days. Every

time he closed his eyes, he found himself back

in the dark tunnel, running toward the

mysterious light and feeling that hot breath on
his neck. As he began to drift off into some kind
of restless sleep, Alex felt himself begin to twist
his wedding ring around. As he fell into the
darkness that is sleep, he saw Liz's face in his
mind.

Alex found himself in the dark tunnel.
This time, the light at the end seemed to be
burning brighter. It was bright enough he could
almost make out the area around him more
than he could before. He inhaled deeply, filling
his nostrils with the smell of damp dirt. He
squinted and slowly turned in a circle. He
looked up and down, trying to get a bearing his
surroundings. He was definitely deep
underground. He had suspected as much all

along. One thing he hadn't noticed before, however, were the metal tracks beneath his feet. They ran in front of him toward the light and also behind him away from it, twisting and turning with the walls of the tunnel.

Alex stared at the ground beneath him for a long time. He focused in on those metal tracks. He was in the mine! He turned back toward the light; that was when he heard the familiar breathing behind him. It was deep with the hint of a growl on the inhale. Instead of running, he stood there and closed his eyes, listening. He matched his breathing to the one behind him. He breathed in deeply, and then exhaled slowly. Alex could feel the hot breath on his neck and all the hairs stood on end. He felt his heartbeat quicken and forced himself to stand still. He felt that hand grab his shoulder and he turned around.

He woke with a start as the road turned from pavement to dirt. The wheels of the Jeep bounced along and the dust swelled all around. Alex looked around the familiar landscape. Last time he drove this road, he was driving and Liz was in the seat next to him. She had been grinning like a kid on their way to Disneyland. He stretched and took a deep breath. The knot in his stomach was tighter than ever and it felt like his heart was beating up in his throat. He looked to his left and noticed even Bob was on high alert. His jaw was set in a hard line and he was tapping his fingers on the steering wheel

104

nervously. They had lost the radio station awhile back so they both sat there in silence, focusing on the road ahead of them. In the distance they could just see the town starting to take shape on the horizon.

As they came over the hill into town, the sky turned dark as night and the rain poured down in sheets. Thunder clapped directly overhead and the lightning struck down from the sky. Alex and Bob cringed as they saw the lightning strike the hillside not far from the cave where Liz disappeared. They peered out the top of the windshield at the foreboding sky and their eyes grew wide. Bob's hands tightened on the steering wheel until his knuckles turned white and he swallowed audibly.

"We need to get out of this shit fast!"

Alex yelled over the sound of the screaming

winds.

Bob nodded in agreement, his eyes

never leaving the road. He pressed the gas

pedal to the floor as they came up to the town.

The Jeep skidded to a stop in front of one of the

abandoned buildings. They jumped out and ran

to the door. Bob turned the handle and pushed,

but nothing happened. The door wouldn't

budge. He looked at Alex and shrugged his

shoulders. Alex waved his hands at him,

signaling him to move out of the way. He

grabbed the handle and rammed the door with

his shoulder. He felt a slight movement. He

repeated this process four times until, finally, the door swung open.

"Holy shit! What the bloody hell is going on out there?!" Bob yelled as he ran his hands through his hair flicking water on the walls and floor in the process.

"Hey, watch the water man!" Alex said shaking his head to attempt to dry out his own hair. He opened his mouth to say something else, but was interrupted by another crash of thunder, followed closely by another streak of lightning not too far from where they were holed up.

They both looked up at the ceiling, then at each other and wordlessly decided to look around. It was a single room cabin with floors

made out of the same wood as the walls. There

was a double bed in the corner by the fireplace.

In the middle of the room was a square wooden

table with four small chairs surrounding it.

There was still a large cast iron pot hanging over

the ashes in the fireplace. Alex walked over to

the table and ran his hand over the newspaper

that was still sitting open on top of the table. He

rubbed his fingers together to get the dust off.

He took a deep breath and coughed. Everything

in the room was covered in a thick layer of a

fine dust.

Neither of them wanted to disturb

anything out of respect for the history, so they

both picked a spot on the floor and leaned

against the wall. The storm raged so loud above

them, that they couldn't hear their own

thoughts, let alone each other. So, they sat in

silence hoping the storm would pass quickly.

Alex leaned his head back against the wall and

closed his eyes. He began to twist his ring

around his finger as thoughts of Liz filled his

head.

They had been dating for almost a year.

He had dropped off the radar as far as his old

colleagues and clients were concerned, and was

in the process of getting his degree in

archeology. While attending classes he also

received quite a bit of hands on training

working digs with Liz and her team. The team,

especially Bob, had been unsure of Alex at the

beginning. They weren't convinced he could or had changed. They were all afraid he was just using Liz and would end up breaking her heart. It took him many months to prove himself to them. Once he did though, he became a part of the family.

It was on a dig that Alex proposed to Liz. He had worked the whole thing out with Bob ahead of time. Bob had distracted Liz while Alex set everything up. He took the ring box and buried it in one of the grids at the dig. Bob came over and told Liz to start digging in one of the grids, but of course it was the wrong one! Alex motioned for him to do something, so Bob told Liz he must be getting old or something and pointed her in the right direction. She laid out all her tools and carefully began to dig. Alex

thought his heart was going to beat right out of

his chest or that he might pee his pants while

he was waiting for her to dig up the ring.

Finally she reached the spot and dug up

the ring box. She gasped and put her hand over

her mouth. She looked around with tears filling

her eyes and found Alex kneeling behind her

with a smile on his face. He took the ring box

from her and opened the lid. The ring was a

gold band with a conservative princess cut

diamond set just above. Her eyes widened and

she looked at him.

"Liz, the day you stormed into my hotel

room in Egypt changed my life. You supported

me when no one else could. You made me want

to be a better man and held my hand while I

began to become one. I never wanted to

answer to or rely on anyone, until you. I want to

lean on you and let you lean on me. And I want

to do it for the rest of our lives. Will you make

me the happiest man alive and be my wife?"

Chapter 14

Alex lifted his head and opened his eyes. The storm had stopped as suddenly as it had begun. The sun was shining through the single dusty window. He look across the room and spotted Bob propped up against the wall, hat pulled down over his eyes, sound asleep yet again. Alex chuckled to himself and shook his head as he pushed himself up from the floor.

"Bob...Bob...BOB!" Bob started as Alex raised his voice. "Wake up old man. The storm has passed, time to get set up."

Bob nodded his head and stretched. His back and knees creaked as he stood up. He twisted left and right to loosen the muscles.

They both shielded their eyes when the stepped out the door into the bright sunlight. They hopped back into the Jeep and drove to the center of town where Liz and Alex had set up the first time they were there.

"This seems to be the best place to set up camp. Liz chose it because it had a clear view of the mountain side and the mine. She figured that way she could keep an eye out to make sure the low life treasure hunters weren't trying to blow anything up. Her words not mine." He clarified at Bob's surprised look. Alex may have gotten out of the game, but many of those treasure hunters were still his friends, or he was still friendly with them.

"She always was a smart girl; tough too. I bet she had those treasure hunters squirming within the first day." Bob said laughing as he pictured little Liz putting those tough guys in their place.

Alex snickered, "Try six hours."

They unloaded the Jeep and got everything set up just as the sun was beginning to sink behind the mountains. Alex started a fire while Bob set up the stove and began unpacking the food they had picked up on the way from the airport. A few years back Bob had found a solar powered refrigerator on a trip back to England. It had changed the face of food on digs. They no longer had to eat nothing but soup and beans; they could bring real food with them and cook meals. He started heating oil on the small propane stove and slicing potatoes for French fries. While he was doing this Alex took the large cast iron pan out and set it on the rocks surrounding the fire to heat it up for the burgers. They said few words, they didn't need them. They had done this so many times; they were a well-oiled machine.

When dinner was ready they each took a chair by the fire and cracked open a beer that was still just barely cold. They ate in comfortable silence. When he had finished his burger, Alex leaned back and looked up at the stars. He loved being in the middle of the desert like that. The stars always seemed brighter and closer there. It reminded him of summer nights spent on the front porch of the cabin with Liz.

He felt more relaxed at that moment than he had been in months. He found it odd that being there in that town made it possible for him to truly relax. He reached down and scratched his ring finger. For some reason the area underneath his wedding ring had been itching all night. He couldn't figure out why. As far as he knew, he hadn't gotten his hands into anything that should have given him a reaction. Alex looked up when he heard Bob grunt.

"I'm going to turn in, been a long day for this old fart." Alex laughed and nodded. He figured that was a good idea and followed suit.

Tomorrow began the real search for Liz. He

hoped to find answers. Hell, he hoped to find

Liz. However, he knew it wouldn't be that easy;

he could feel it in his bones.

Chapter 15

That night, instead of the dark tunnel,

Alex found himself in an open room surrounded

by a strange bright white light. Even though it

was possibly the brightest light he had ever

seen, he didn't feel the need to shield his eyes

from it. His heart was pounding so loud it was

all he could hear. The light enveloped him. He

turned his head to look around, but all he could

see was the white light.

His head began to pound and his ring

finger itched so bad there was a burning

sensation. He tried to reach down and scratch

it, but he found that he couldn't move. Alex

closed his eyes and took deep breaths, hoping it

would stop the pounding in his head. His eyes
shot open when he heard his name whispered
through the light.

"Alex....Aaaalex...." He tried to look
around, but still couldn't move. The voice
seemed to be moving closer. "Alex..."

"Liz! Liz is that you honey?" He tried
desperately to find her in the light; his eyes
darting back and forth frantically. "Liz, where
are you? I can't find you....I need you back,
baby! Tell me what to do."

"Alex, you have the answer. You've
always had the answer."

"What are talking about? I don't know
anything."

Her laugh echoed around him. He smiled and closed his eyes, drinking in the sound he had missed so much. A tear trailed down his cheek and he opened his eyes as her laugh began to fade away into the white light.

"Liz, don't go…Please, don't leave me."

He woke up in his tent, his cheeks still damp and his eyes filled with unshed tears. He ran his hands down his face and sighed. He needed to get up and tell Bob about his dream, but he just couldn't bring himself to move yet. He lay there thinking about what Liz had said. *What did she mean I had the answer? How do I have the answer when I have no idea what I'm doing? How does that help me find her? Liz, this*

121

was not the best time for one of your mysterious riddles! I needed your help!

He sat up more frustrated than ever. They had come all the way out to California to find answers, to find where Liz was. He felt no closer to finding her than he had before. He didn't assume the answer would magically come to him, but he simply had no idea where to start. He let out a deep guttural growl and ran his hands through his hair. He got up and got dressed. He found Bob sitting by the fire pit and having a cup of coffee. When Bob saw Alex coming, he leaned forward and filled a cup with the thick, black brew and held it out. Alex took the cup from him gratefully.

"You look like shite."

"Thanks buddy. That's so nice of you to say."

"Sorry, just thought I'd be honest. What's going on?" Bob asked chuckling.

Alex took a sip of his coffee and told Bob about the dream he had the night before. He told him everything, the white light, the burning sensation in his ring finger, and Liz. As he was hearing himself retell the dream he knew sounded crazier and crazier. But, he couldn't stop talking; it all seemed to spill out. When he had finished he couldn't even look at Bob. He was afraid he would think he was as crazy as he felt, pack up his stuff and leave him there in the desert.

"So what did she mean about you having the answer?" Alex looked up, surprised.

"You don't think I'm crazy?"

"I think you're out of your mind. But, I also believe there is something going on here that is completely out of our power. So...What did she mean?"

"Well, in true Liz fashion, she left me with more questions than answers. I have no idea what she was talking about. If I had the answer, don't you think I would have found her already?"

Bob sat back, sipped his coffee and studied Alex. It was so hard not being able to help him. He wasn't used to not having answers. Bob had always been smart; he was the top of the class in both high school and college. He had quickly moved up the ladder in the archeology field and had been the youngest person to become head of the research department at a prestigious museum in New York. He had held that position for over twenty years now and had always had the answers he needed when he needed them. Liz was the most promising member of his team; he knew she would take over for him one day when he was finally ready to retire. Not knowing how to help her was more frustrating than anything else he had ever experienced. He watched

everyday as Alex moved closer and closer to the

edge and he wasn't sure how to keep him from

falling off.

Chapter 16

Liz held her head and took a few deep breaths. She knew going to Alex was a risk, but she had never expected it to take so much out of her. She had to find someplace to hide before any of the others found her. She needed time to recover and couldn't do it just anywhere. She had been caught in this parallel universe some kind of time loop for seven months now and she knew what these people were capable of.

She had known this was her destiny long before she had convinced Alex to go to California with her. As soon as she had found out that is where the artifact lay she knew she had to go and be the one to find it. She had felt

guilty all those weeks they were searching and

digging because she couldn't tell Alex the truth.

But, it was imperative that he believed it was

just another dig. If he had known the truth, he

would have tried to stop her and the reality was

she probably would have let him. Every time

she closed her eyes she saw his face. She saw

the furrow on his brow that he only got when

he was worried about her or upset with her.

And she knew right now he was a little bit of

both.

Liz had always been special. She knew

from an early age that she simply wasn't like

the other kids. By age seven, she could see

things, things that she shouldn't be able to see

and knew things that she should not know. At first she had no control over it, and it had frightened her. The images would suddenly flood her mind in waves. It would take everything out of her and leave her with a pounding headache for hours. She was afraid every minute that another vision was going to come over her. Finally after years of trying to fight it or cure it, her parents gave up and accepted that something special was happening to their little girl.

The summer she turned ten they sent her to stay with her great grandmother. She was surprised when her parents had told her their plans. In all her years she had never heard her mother talk about her grandmother, let alone met her. But, she didn't have much say in the matter and two days after school let out they put her on a train to the Louisiana Bayou. When she got there, she discovered a world so different from the one she lived in. It was hotter than anything she had ever experienced and everyone talked different. However, it didn't take long for her to discover, for the first time, she felt like she truly belonged.

She spent that summer learning from her great grandmother and honing her gift. That was the biggest lesson she learned; her visions were a gift. Her parents had spent years making her feel like there was something wrong with her or that she was cursed. But, Meme had told her that a gift like that was only a curse if you let it be. It was then that Liz chose to embrace her gift and learn to control it rather than let it control her.

It was that gift that had led her to Alex's hotel room that night in Egypt. In all the years they had been together, she had never been able to come out and tell him about it. She knew he had his suspicions because he had asked questions at first. But, she had either changed the subject or lashed out at him. Eventually the questions stopped. She had never told anyone about her secret and just could never seem to find the words to tell Alex; even though he was the first one she had ever wanted to tell. Her gift had taken her far in her career and led her to the love of her life.

Although, she'd always known fate would lead
her to Alex. Without Alex she could never fulfill
her destiny...

Liz dove to the ground and covered her
head as shots and then an explosion rang out
through the air. She waited for the dust to
settle around her and then forced herself to her
feet and continued to run as fast as she could.
When she finally reached the cave, the same
cave she had been in when this was all set in to
motion only in a different time and place, she
stumbled inside and went as far back as she
could. She found the first aid kit and water she
had stashed there weeks ago and popped the
top to the aspirin bottle. She swallowed a few
pills and lay back against the cool stone. She

knew she was safe here, none of the others could see it; they didn't even know it was there.

She closed her eyes, hoping to drift off into a deep sleep to regain her strength before the next wave hit. It didn't take long before she could feel her body being taken over by sleep. The words of the curse that had shown Liz her destiny many years ago echoed in her head as she gave in and drifted off.

She whose mind is true,

And whose heart is pure

Must be lost despite herself.

True love will find its strength within,

To be rejoined,

And break the curse for all eternity.

Chapter 17

Alex and Bob had decided they needed to start looking around for clues that would lead them to rescue Liz. Bob wanted to start in the cave where Alex knew Liz had been last. The forces at work had different plans though, when they started toward the hill that led up to the cave, Alex felt something pulling him toward the mine instead. He tried to resist it, but it was as though there was something physically holding onto him pulling him toward the entrance to the mine.

"Alex? Hey, Alex, where are you going?" Bob called out to him, but Alex didn't hear him. He appeared to be in a trance. Whatever was pulling him toward the mine wouldn't let him

even turn his head to look at Bob. He could just

make out the sound of footsteps running

behind him. It was a déjà vu of his dreams, his

heart began pounding and he couldn't look

behind him, but he wasn't sure he wanted to

either. Something was behind him, catching up

quickly.

He felt a hand on his shoulder and

yelled. The hand forced him around, snapping

him out of his trance and Alex breathed a sigh

of relief when he realized it was Bob. He shook

his head to clear it. Bob's hand was still

clenching his shoulder; Alex grabbed his

forearm to steady himself and nodded. Alex

coughed, he felt as if he had been suffocating.

When Alex was able to catch his breath, he and
Bob took off running back toward their camp
site. When they reached the site he took his
beat up khaki back pack off and dropped it on
the dusty ground as he collapsed into one of the
chairs by the fire pit.

He held his head in his hand and rubbed
his temples. His head was pounding. He used
his thumb on his left hand to move his ring
around so he could scratch underneath it. His
finger was itching so bad it was burning again.
There was something in him telling him to rip
the ring off and throw it across the desert, that
it would give him some relief. He almost gave
into the voice inside, but right as he was about
to take his ring off Bob handed him a metal cup

filled part way with an amber liquid. He took a
sip and let the whiskey glide down his throat,
reveling in the warm feeling that filled his body
as it hit his stomach. He leaned back in his chair
and breathed deep.

Bob sat across from him and slowly
sipped the whiskey he had poured for himself.
His hands were shaking and he could tell that
Alex was shaken as well. Bob gave him a couple
of minutes to decompress before he tried to
talk to him. At first he wasn't even sure what to
say to Alex.

"What the bloody hell was that?" He
raised his eyebrows as Alex looked over at him
and shook his head.

"Your guess is as good as mine. I felt like I had no control over my body. My feet were moving, but I wasn't telling them where to go. Even turning my head to look at you was impossible and I couldn't hear you talking to me. It was like I was surrounded by white noise. I was practically suffocating under the pressure of the powerful force that was holding me." Alex closed his eyes and didn't even realize that he was scratching under his ring again.

"What's going on there?" Bob asked gesturing toward Alex's hand.

"Not sure, it's been itching like crazy since we got here."

Bob furrowed his brow. There were no plants around that Alex could have touched that would give him that kind of reaction and as far as he knew Alex couldn't have been bitten by any bugs. They were in the middle of the desert, after all. He stood up and walked over to Alex. He made a motion for Alex to show him his hand. Alex obliged and held his left hand out for Bob to examine. Bob turned Alex's hand over and shifted his ring up and down on his finger. There was no rash and no bug bites; he could find no explanation as to why it would be itching that badly. Bob gave Alex a look of uncertainty as he let go of his hand.

"I'm going to get some dinner going, any requests?" Alex shrugged his shoulders and closed his eyes. Bob took it for what it was and

went to find something to make for dinner.

Chapter 18

Alex forced himself to eat something.
He wasn't even sure what it was that he was
eating; everything tasted like cardboard. When
he couldn't force another bite down, he stood
up and told Bob he was heading to bed. It was
early and still light out, but Alex's head was
throbbing and he couldn't stand another
minute in the bright sunlight. He splashed some
not so cold water on his face before ducking
into his tent.

It was so hot in the tent that he
immediately stripped down to his underwear
and laid on top of his sleeping bag. He covered
his eyes with his arm and hoped that sleep

would take over quickly. He couldn't escape the

pounding behind his eyes and in his ears. As he

lay there every inch of his body became covered

in sweat. He sighed and crossed the tent to

open the flap hoping to get a breeze blowing

inside. It seemed to help a little bit and he lay

back down. He turned on his side, facing the

wall and closed his eyes again.

He must have fallen asleep because he

soon found himself in the dark once more. The

moist, dusty smell had become all too familiar

and barely even burned his nostrils anymore.

His frustration level was boiling over at this

point. He had flown all the way to California and

suffered the desert heat; he was still no closer

to finding Liz or getting answers. The dreams

seemed to have followed him here and he still

didn't know what they were telling him. His

head was still pounding and, to top it off, his

finger was itching and burning; he couldn't get

that to stop either. He reached down to scratch

the finger and decided he had enough and was

going to just take his ring off. He pulled and

pulled, but the ring wouldn't budge.

Alex couldn't even see his hand in front

of his face; he licked his finger around the ring

and pulled again. It wouldn't budge. He sighed,

and then laughed. *What are you doing you*

idiot? This is a dream, even if it did come off, it's

not like it would really affect anything! Pull it

together. You're no good to Liz if you unravel.

He rubbed his hands down his face and over the

stubble on his chin. He could feel the affects the stress had on him. He was so distracted that he hadn't even noticed, no wonder Bob looked so worried every time he looked at him. Alex realized his cheeks had become sunk in. He felt around the rest of his body and noticed, while it was still muscular, it had grown gaunt and thin as well. How had he let things get this bad? This was not who he was and Liz would never forgive him for letting his own health go trying to find her.

Dude, you are such a pussy. The man Liz fell in love with does not let life get in the way of him accomplishing anything. When are you going to stop being so stubborn and actually start listening. Your whining and self-pity have got to stop. You have the answers, Liz said so.

Snap out of it and get your shit together.

Alex opened his eyes and found himself in his tent. He was inside his sleeping bag and there was a damp cloth on his forehead. He slid it off and slowly sat up. His head had stopped pounding and he was starving. He felt like he hadn't eaten in days. He made use of the wash station set up in one corner of his tent and quickly dressed. When he glanced at his watch, he realized it was late afternoon. He couldn't believe he had slept that long, why hadn't Bob woken him up? He wasn't sure he really cared right now, all he could think about was finding something to eat; he took the low grumble as agreement from his stomach and stepped out into the desert sun.

He walked directly over to the kitchen area and began rummaging for something to eat. He looked up and found Bob sitting at a makeshift table pouring over books and notes. He looked a little worse for the wear and Alex couldn't figure out how that had happened in one night. He made himself a sandwich and grabbed a bottle of water, then carried it over to where Bob was sitting. Bob jumped and looked up as Alex sat down across from him.

"Bloody hell, Alex. You're up!?" Alex was confused by Bob's reaction. He knew he had slept late, but that seemed a little dramatic even for him. He chuckled as he took a long

drink from his bottle; why was he so thirsty?

"Bob? You okay, buddy?" Alex asked as

he began to inhale his sandwich. He couldn't

believe how hungry he was.

"Alex, I don't know how to tell you this.

You've been asleep for three bloody days."

Alex stopped eating and looked up a

Bob. Three days? How was that possible? He

slowly continued eating, but the confused look

remained on his face. He couldn't wrap his head

around the fact that he had slept for three days

straight. It did explain a few things, like his

insatiable hunger, but he couldn't fathom that

three days had passed.

"I wanted to take you to the nearest hospital when you didn't wake up. But, when I got you into the Jeep and tried to leave town…I couldn't! It wouldn't let me leave with you. As I reached the town limit, the Jeep spun out and I almost lost control completely. I turned around and booked it back here. All I could do was put you back in your tent and try to keep you as cool as possible. If you hadn't woken up today I wasn't sure what I was going to do. Bollocks…I was so bloody scared. I bloody hate not knowing what to do." Alex didn't know what to say to that, so instead he nodded toward the books on the table.

"Have you found anything, like what attacked me right before I was in a three day coma?" Alex tried to keep his voice light, but he knew Bob could see the worry in his eyes. Finished eating, Alex sat back and worked on his second bottle of water while he listened.

"Well, in between trying to find a way to get you out of here and making sure you weren't dead, I went through ever book from cover to cover. I reread all of our notes for the hundredth time. I even walked around some. Of course, I couldn't go far due to your sorry ass being laid up in there." Bob said as motioned toward the tent. "There's nothing, absolutely bloody nothing. We've been here for a bloody week and are still no closer than we were when we arrived. All we have to show for it, is you being in a bloody three day coma!"

Alex could tell the last three days had taken their toll on Bob. He walked around the table and put his hand on Bob's shoulder, giving it a light squeeze. Bob dropped his head into his hands. Alex knew he felt defeated; they both did. He had an idea of what he needed to do, but first he had to get Bob to get some rest.

Chapter 19

Alex knew that Bob had hardly slept in the past three days and his body must be feeling the effects. Alex had to reassure Bob multiple times that he was fine and then practically push him into his tent in order to get him to go. Alex waited until he was sure that Bob was asleep before readying himself for what needed to happen.

He couldn't simply sit and wait for Bob to wake up. He had never experienced a time when he was unable to find the answers he needed. Since he had started treasure hunting all those years ago, the answers had always shown themselves to him. This was the first time he had to deal with the frustration of not

knowing how to get what he wanted.

Alex grabbed his trusty khaki back pack

and his lucky hat. He could no longer sit around

and wait for the answers to appear to him. He

was going to find Liz and he was going to find

her today; he had to. He took off toward the

cave.

He was glad Bob had been there to help

him, but, he had a feeling finding the true

answers was something he was going to have to

do on his own. He scratched his finger and spun

his ring around while he walked. There was

something eerie about walking through the

small empty town alone. Everything was quite,

everything except the ravens. Each building Alex

passed had ravens lining the roof top. He swore

they were following him. Their manic screeches

echoed off the hills that surrounded the town

and sent chills down Alex's spine. He looked up

and saw the ravens' beady black eyes staring

back at him. Alex shivered and forced himself to

keep walking. He could see the cave getting

closer, and with each step the ravens' calls grew

louder and then suddenly stopped all together.

As he neared the base of the trail that

lead up to the cave he gave one last glance over

his shoulder and saw that while their cries had

quieted, each raven was still watching his every

move. He began to feel powerful pull toward

the mine again. Just like before, it was as if

something was physically pulling him in that direction. He tried to fight it. He did everything he could to resist. He was convinced the answers he was looking for lay in the cave. Eventually, he sighed and realized that fighting is what put him out for three days. He had lost all that time because he was fighting the forces at work. He decided that resistance was futile and gave into the mysterious force that was leading him toward the mine.

As he neared the mine the force that was pulling him seemed to loosen its grip on him. He had more control over his body than he had before. He stopped just long enough to get his flashlight out of his pack. Readjusting it on his shoulders, he checked the batteries and inched closer. As he reached the entrance of

the mine he took a deep breath. He could feel

his heart beating faster inside his chest as the

adrenaline began to pulse through his body. He

glanced up before he entered and noticed one

lone raven sitting on top of a wooden beam

above the entrance watching him.

Chapter 20

Liz woke with a start. She looked

around the cave. She was alone; the same way

she had been when she fell asleep. But, there

was a presence that she knew so well and had

longed for all these months she had been

trapped. It was Alex. She could feel him, she

could almost smell him. The musty smell that

was completely *him* hung faintly in the air,

blowing in on the breeze.

She breathed in deeply, savoring the

scent. She could feel her heart aching with each

breath she took that was filled with him. She

knew he wasn't here, it was impossible for him

to be. But, she closed her eyes and could feel

his strong arms wrapped around her. She

leaned her head back and could feel his

muscular chest underneath it and even hear his

heart beating. She opened her eyes and wiped

away the tears that threatened to spill over. She

couldn't lose it, not now. If she was feeling him

that strongly, he must have finally set his

stubbornness aside and be close to figuring

things out.

She had known this day would come.

She had been patiently waiting for these long

seven months. He was so hard headed that she

knew he had to figure things out on his own.

Not even the powers at work both here and in

the parallel world he was in would have been

able to force him in anyway. She had felt her

belief waning when he had slipped into the coma. But, she had never given up on him before and she wouldn't start now. He would find what he needed to find and he would bring her back. She knew it in her soul.

If he was that close, though, it meant she had to hurry. There was no time to waist. She had to be in exactly the right spot when he got there or she would be lost to this parallel world forever; doomed to relive the horrible time loop for all eternity. She refused to let that happen. She knew it was her destiny to come here, but she didn't have to stay.

She gathered her stuff up and headed to the front of the cave. It was dark out; she paused at the entrance and listened. Everything

was quiet...for now. She pulled the chain out of

her shirt. On the end of it was her wedding ring.

Usually it never left her finger. But, when she

had ended up here she had quickly realized that

it put her in danger. The majority of the people

who were dragged here by the curse were the

definition of evil. They would kill you just for the

sheer pleasure of killing, but if they saw you had

something valuable you would be more of a

target. She had taken it off and put it on the

chain around her neck. She couldn't lose it. She

listened again; still quiet. She kissed the ring,

stuck it back inside her shirt and crept out of

the cave and down the path. As she reached the

bottom of the hill, she looked down the moonlit

street running through the town. It was quiet

except for the ravens lining the roof tops and

calling out to her. Liz studied them for a

moment and shivered as a chill ran up her

spine.

Chapter 21

"Here we go…Move…Take a

step…Dammit, Alex, move your feet!"

He was glad there was no one else

around, he was sure he sounded insane talking

to himself. But, it was the only way for him to

get his feet to work. He slowly entered the

mine, his trusty flashlight leading the way. He

really wasn't sure what he was looking for, but

deep down he knew the answer was in

here…somewhere.

After he had been walking for a few

minutes, he stopped, his brow furrowed. He

shined the light on his left hand and stared at it.

He was confused. The good news was, it had

stopped itching. On the other hand, it appeared that the deeper into the mine he walked, his wedding ring was starting to vibrate. He had thought he noticed something different at the entrance, but he had shrugged it off and hadn't thought anything more of it. Now he couldn't ignore it anymore. He could feel the vibration all the way up his arm.

They had argued over those rings. The simple gold band was perfect for Alex, he didn't need anything special. However, he felt that since money was not an issue, Liz should have the ring he felt she deserved. She didn't feel the same way and had told him to take the ring he proposed with back. Her insistence on it had infuriated him.

"But, Alex I don't need a big ring."

"I know you don't *need* it, but doesn't every girl secretly want a nice big diamond on her finger? Hell, Liz, would it kill you to just be grateful?"

"When have you ever known me to be like other girls?" Alex nodded in agreement and laughed at himself, he wasn't sure why he had gotten so mad, it was her ring after all. He didn't know what he had been thinking in the first place. He held up his hand to stop her before she could say anything more.

"I know, I know. How can you do your job with a giant diamond on your finger? You would never wear it. Why spend that much

money on something that will just sit in a
jewelry box? I get it."

That night he was sitting on the porch,
drinking a beer when she came to him with a
small wooden box in her hands. She silently
handed it to him as she took her seat next to
him. He opened the lid and saw two matching
simple gold bands sitting inside. He looked up at
her with his questions written all over his face.

"These were my great grandparent's
rings. They wore them for almost sixty years. I
feel like they might be good luck. They are
special, you see." Alex nodded and put his arm
around her. He pulled her close to him and
kissed the top of her head.

165

The Curse

He propped the flashlight under his arm
and pulled off his ring. This time it slid off
without an issue. He held it in the light and
examined it. He had worn this ring on his hand
for the better part of a decade and it was like he
was seeing it for the first time. Here in this
mine, an engraving he had never noticed before
seemed to light up. It was in some sort of
ancient language he had never seen before.
Even though he didn't recognize the language
his heart to him what it said *True love will find
its strength from within.* From the beginning Liz
had told him that their rings were special. He
had always figured she simply meant they were
good luck charms because her great
grandparents had had such a successful

marriage. Now he was beginning to realize that

somehow he knew something like this would

happen one day. She, and possibly even her

great grandparents, had prepared them for it

with those rings.

Chapter 22

Bob awoke as the sun was setting behind the hills. For the first time in days he felt refreshed and ready for anything. He washed and dressed. As he stepped outside his tent and looked around, he realized that maybe he wasn't ready for 'anything' after all. He had not been ready to step out and not find Alex there. He rushed over to the table where his books and notes were neatly stacked. There was no note and Alex's pack was gone.

"Dammit, Alex!" Bob shouted in frustration. He knew exactly where he had gone. He should have known that Alex wouldn't wait for him. Bob had that feeling in the pit of his stomach; the feeling of doom. He had reservations about going after Alex with night setting in soon, but he couldn't simply leave him out there either.

With a deep sigh, Bob grabbed his pack and his hat and set out. He dug his flashlight out of his pack as he walked at a quick pace. Alex had a huge head start; he probably left hours ago. He shined the light on his hand to check the batteries and gave a quick, satisfied nod. They had been headed for the cave the other day when Alex was taken over. That was where Bob's gut was telling him to go. Whatever had taken a hold of Alex had pulled him toward the mine, but Bob was sure he would have fought it again.

The cave is the last place Liz was before she disappeared. Bob was convinced that was where the answer lay. All the way to the split where the path wound up the hill toward the cave and through town for the mine Bob argued within himself. Reality was, he had no idea which way Alex would have gone. He had seen how fighting the forces had taken everything out of him, so maybe he had given into them and let them lead him to the mine.

"Alex! Alex, mate , can you hear me?" He shouted out as he reached the split. He hesitated there for a moment. Dusk was setting in, so he turned his flashlight on and shone it back and forth down each path. He wished there was some sort of sign to tell him which

170

way to go. His sign came as he took one single step in the direction of the mine.

Whatever force had dragged Alex in that direction threw him in the opposite. It was the force of a dozen men pushing against his chest and throwing him through the air. He felt his feet leave the ground and travelled through the air for what seemed like an eternity. He landed about four feet back the way he had come with an audible thud. All the breath he didn't know he had been holding rushed out of him in a sudden woosh. He lay in the dirt trying to find his breath again as the stars came out and night took over the desert.

"Well, I guess I won't be going that way." He whispered aloud as he finally caught his breath again. He groaned as he slowly sat up and gently placed his hand on his rib cage. He carefully lifted his shirt; there were welts and dark bruises already appearing on his chest and rib cages. He was pretty sure he had more than one broken rib. He growled in frustration and let his shirt fall back down. He clenched his teeth together and pushed himself up.

Bob gingerly bent over and retrieved his flashlight. Surprisingly it was still working just fine. He held it in a shaky hand and placed the other one protectively over his broken ribs. He shined the light down the path leading through town to the mine shaft one last time before

172

heading up the hill toward the cave. Since he

couldn't get past the forces guarding the mine,

he would head up to the cave and see if there

was any way for him to help from there.

Chapter 23

Liz crept through the town, using only the moon to guide her. She didn't dare turn on her flashlight for fear of drawing attention to herself. She glanced up at the ravens on the rooftops and prayed that their cries would not disturb the others and alert them to her presence. Everyone was quiet at the moment, but it wouldn't last long.

She knew she had a few hours before things began to get crazy again. When she first got here, she had timed it. Every seven hours the time loop started again and lasted thirty-seven minutes before it reset. People were drawn to the town by the artifact, which fed on their greed. But, that was just a curtain hiding what truly lay in that town. It was a curse. Most of the people that were drawn there had done something irreprehensible in their lifetime, maybe more than one thing. The curse pulled them into the parallel world and doomed them to relieve their greatest offense over and over again for all eternity. It was a special kind of purgatory for the truly wicked.

She didn't belong here. She knew that. But, she also knew it was her destiny to be sucked in with the others. Without her being here, Alex would never break the curse. Of course she felt that these people needed to be punished. The things she had witnessed in the past seven months, she would never forget.

175

But, no one deserved this; reliving these awful moments over and over again. People died here only to be brought back and killed again hours later.

She was half way through town when she heard movement behind her. She quickly moved into the shadows of the building nearby. There were still a few hours until all hell broke loose again, but that didn't mean anyone of them wouldn't kill you just because you were standing there. She pressed herself up against the side of the building and held her breath until the man stumbled by. There was no shortage of liquor here either and the men made good use of it. For some reason the curse was more for men than women. She had been here seven months and had discovered she was the only woman here. That made it even more important for her to stay out of sight, who knew what they would do to her if they discovered she was here.

She had found evidence that the curse didn't always separate the evil and the innocent though. Deep down she knew that many innocent lives had been lost to this curse when it had taken over the town. How else could you explain the way the town was left during the gold rush or what happened to all the others when it had taken her? The part she didn't understand is what happened to those innocent souls when they are taken. It seemed like when the time loop reset itself, any innocents that were lost during the chaos, stayed lost. They didn't reset like the rest did. She had tried and tried to find them, but couldn't find more than a few articles of clothing or memorabilia that showed they had been here. It was the teddy bear laying in the dirt she found about week after she arrived that had broken her heart the most.

"Come on, Alex, be there." She whispered into the dark as she arrived at the mouth of the mine shaft. She held onto her ring which had started vibrating and glowing as soon as Alex had entered the mine on his end. She closed her eyes, took a deep breath and took the first step inside.

Chapter 24

Bob reached the top of the hill and leaned against the entrance of the cave. He rested his hand on his ribs and took deep breaths, trying to keep the nausea at bay. The pain was so severe he was afraid he would throw up, pass out or both and none of those options helped Alex and Liz. He closed his eyes and slowly counted to ten while breathing deep and letting it out slowly. The pain was still there, but he no longer felt like he was going to lose what little was in his stomach.

He pushed himself away from the rock wall and shone his flashlight into the cave. The light began to flicker and then went out completely. He shook it and the cave lit up once more. But, it only took a few seconds for the bulb to flicker and die again. Bob hit the flashlight against his hand to try to shake the batteries into working again.

"Bloody useless torch..." He growled as he set his pack on the ground and squatted to try to dig out more batteries, wincing all the way down. He found two lonely batteries at the very bottom of his pack and kissed them before dumping the old ones out and replacing them. He carefully stood up and swung his pack back over his shoulders. The flashlight working once more, he took a cautious first step into the cave. Part of him was afraid he would be thrown back again, and he wasn't sure his body would handle that very well.

Nothing happened. There was no electric shock and no throwing. He breathed a sigh of relief and started forward. He shined the light in front of him, but there seemed to be no end to the cave. He saw nothing but a dark endless tunnel stretching in front of him. There was no sign that Liz had been here digging or otherwise. He had no idea where she was when she found the artifact and disappeared. He didn't even know if he was going to be able to do any good from up here at all. But, he had to try.

Chapter 25

Alex couldn't remember a time he felt like such a dumbass. He had been wandering around the mine for hours. He would take a tunnel and circle back around to where he was. He was getting nowhere. Then it hit him. The ring was telling him where to go. The engraving lit up brighter when he was heading in the right direction, and the closer he got the stronger the vibration got. Finally, he held the ring up in front of him and followed the glow.

He silently berated himself for being so stupid and wasting so much time. It wasn't exactly GPS, but it was better than wandering around blind. It seemed as though the tunnels kept multiplying and changing. Every time he circled back around to the center, it seemed either there were more tunnels or that they were in different positions than they were the first time. He went through a series of tunnels and came out into an opening.

"Dammit! What is wrong with this place?" He shouted in frustration. The opening was a round room, surrounded on all sides by tunnels leading in different directions. The biggest problem was that the ring didn't seem stop vibrating and glowing until he had taken a few steps into a tunnel. This meant he had to back track to the main room and start over again. The frustration was forming a tight knot in his stomach and he clenched his jaw down until his teeth hurt.

His gut was telling him that he didn't have time for this and that sent his anger through the roof. His impatience caused him to ignore the ring and take his own path. That was the first mistake he made. He let his ego take over his body and lost his trust in the tools Liz had given him. It wasn't until he was literally stopped in his tracks that he began to realize his mistake.

"Son of a….What the hell?" He stuttered out as he stumbled backward and tried to regain his footing. When he was able to stand still again, and the flashlight he had dropped stopped spinning around he looked up and couldn't believe what he was seeing. Standing in front of him in the middle of the tunnel was an ancient guardian. He had assumed that since the artifact supposedly had an Egyptian back ground, that the whole thing centered around the Egyptians. But, looking at this guardian he could see how wrong he was. That must have been why he couldn't find any answers; they had been looking in the wrong direction the whole time.

The guy in front of him was of unrecognizable origins. He wore a long robe with the hood pulled up, so the shadows fell over his face which was tilted down, looking at the floor. He was taller than Alex and broader

as well. He held a staff in his hand that seemed
to have a blue glow, similar to the one coming
from Alex's ring, to it in the dark tunnel. Alex
took one step forward and the Guardian pushed
the hood off his head, revealing a strong
completely bald head and pale skinned face
that was smooth and wrinkle free. When he
slowly raised his eyes to meet Alex's they were
so dark they could only be described as black.
The Guardian slowly crouched into a defensive
position, his legs spread wide and the hand with
the staff raised above his head. The other hand
was out in front of him as if to tell Alex to stop.

At first that's exactly what Alex did. He
froze right where he was. This may have been
one of those times he should have listened to

head that was telling him to turn around and run. However, that's not what he did. Instead he listened to his heart that was telling him that this guy was keeping him from getting to Liz. Those thoughts forced his frustration level that was already high to boil over and he was no longer thinking clearly. He didn't turn around, pick up his flashlight and run. He did, however, charge the Guardian.

Chapter 26

Liz didn't have the same problems navigating the mine as Alex did. She understood the power of the rings and was able to utilize it right away. She pulled it out of her shirt and let the chain hang down. Its glow was so bright; she almost didn't need the flashlight in her hand. She was in a hurry, but knew better than to rush too much. Rushing caused mistakes, and she didn't have the time to make them. She cautiously navigated the tunnels, moving deeper and deeper into the mine.

She had come here one other time when she was first pulled into this world. She quickly found being here, in the mine, at the wrong time was more dangerous than being outside. Unseen forces were everywhere pushing and pulling her. She had barely been able to escape that first time and had sworn she wouldn't go back until the time came that she had to. Now was that time, she knew it, but that didn't make her feel any less unsettled about having to be that deep in the mine.

Right after making her way out of the mine that first time, she had ran into a group of people that had obviously been trapped here for a while. No one there really knew what had happened to them or how long they had been there. But, she could tell the ones that had been there the longest. There eyes had darkened and they had lost their souls over the long years fighting to survive and reliving the horrible things in their lives and others. The ones that surrounded her as she came out of the mine that day had been there for a very long time.

Her heart started pounding and she felt her palms begin to sweat. Her breath quickened and she looked around for an escape route. She found none. She was surrounded. She was grateful Alex had made her take all those kickboxing classes over the years. She just hoped she could remember the things she had learned. She knew if she had any chance of getting out this, she was going to have to strike hard and fast. She closed her eyes, took a deep breath in and slowly let it out. When she opened her eyes, she surveyed the situation.

Ok, three guys. They are all bigger than you and none of them have anything to lose. Their instinct is to harm. The one to your right is limping, favoring his left knee. The one to your left can't seem to focus on anything for more than a minute, his eyes are constantly moving and he's squinting like he lost his glasses. The one in front of you must be the ring leader though. No obvious weaknesses and he hasn't stopped staring at you since you came out of the mine. Breath….Focus….You can do this.

She took another deep breath and went for it. She was able to see each move seconds before it happened. The one to her left came at her; she ducked low and kicked out making contact with the other guy's weak knee. 'Weak

Knee' went down screaming in pain. She

popped back up and punched the leader

directly in his gut; knocking the wind out of him.

It didn't stall him for long, but it was long

enough for her to distract the third guy and he

never saw her roundhouse kick coming, she

connected with his head and he saw nothing

but black. She stood in a defensive position

waiting for the leader to attack. She knew if she

timed it right she could use his weight against

him. He came at her and she turned and used

his own momentum to flip him over. He fell

hard on his back and she heard the breath rush

out of him. She didn't wait around to see if they

were going to get back up. She headed straight

for the cave; hoping to find a place to hide out

for a while. That was when she discovered that on this side, the mine was shielded from those who were there. No one except her could see the entrance. She was lying low just inside the cave when she heard the group of guys coming up the path, looking for her. Her heart was pounding and she had to force her breathing to slow so they didn't hear her. However, when they reached the area where the cave was, they paused to look around and simply bypassed it. She breathed a sigh of relief as they walked away and knew she could use that to her advantage.

This time the mine felt very different. She could still feel those forces at work, but they were no longer pushing her and trying to force her to leave. It felt as if they were

propelling her forward this time. She did find it

odd though; she had expected some sort of

resistance once she entered the mine. But, so

far, there was nothing. Occasionally she felt the

slightest tug from whatever the forces working

there were; it had been an easy ride thus far.

That worried her more than if she had been met

with resistance right away. That's when she saw

him; the Guardian.

Chapter 27

Bob looked around the cave. He squinted into the darkness ahead. There was a flickering, like someone was watching television around the corner. He inched closer to the strange glow, forcing his feet to work. He felt his heart up in his throat and could hear it pounding in his ears. He took a deep breath and let it out slowly; trying to calm his heart before it beat right out of his body.

"Alright Bobby old boy, you can do this. You're not too old for this shit. You still have a few more go rounds in you. Now move it!" He nodded his head in agreement with his own pep talk and winced, placing a hand on his ribs and he continued forward, toward the flickering

light. He slowly made his way through the cave.

He reached the back where it curved toward

the light and paused again. He leaned against to

cool stone wall, put his head back and closed his

eyes. His head was pounding and every time he

moved pain shot throughout his entire body

starting at his ribs.

For a second he thought about how

easy it would be to turn around and leave the

cave. He could make his way down to the

campsite, pack up his stuff, get in the Jeep and

take off. He could make his way to the nearest

town with a hospital and put the whole thing

behind him. He could live the rest of his days

denying any of this ever happened. He

entertained the thought for no more than a second or two, however. He loved Liz like a sister; from the day she had walked into his office, fresh faced newly graduated and eager, she had been there for him. She was the one that had held his hand as his wife lay in the hospital dying of a terminal illness. She was the one that stood by him at the funeral. Alex had grown to be as close as a brother. He couldn't desert them now.

He pulled out the St. Michael pendent he always wore around his neck and kissed it before pushing off the wall. He hadn't been to church since his wife died, but his roots ran deep. His mother's family had been devout Catholics and in many ways that had never left him. He prayed that St. Michael would protect him and poked his head around the corner. He was surprised to find the room empty. It was dark except for the strange flickering light that was coming from the other side of the wall.

He cautiously stepped around the corner into a round open room. He turned toward the light and couldn't believe what he was seeing. On the wall there were images being projected from nowhere. Two separate live images side by side. He stood frozen in disbelief. How was it even possible? It was Alex down in the mine charging a man in a robe, but on the other side was Liz in what looked like the same mine in front of the same robed man. He watched for a moment as everything began clicking into place. But, could hit be true? Could

that be where Liz was this whole time?

"Bloody..hell."

Chapter 28

Alex went straight for the Guardian. But, he wasn't quite quick enough and the Guardian easily dodged his attack. Alex's momentum sent him running into the opposite wall with enough force to knock the wind out of him for a minute. In that time the Guardian could have easily attacked him, but he didn't. He simply stood there while Alex caught his breath.

Once Alex did find his breath again, he looked at the Guardian and at the now unguarded tunnel. He smirked and turned around to head down in the direction he had wanted to go. But, just as he turned to leave, the Guardian was suddenly standing in front of him once again blocking his path.

"What the hell?" Alex said as he looked behind him and then at the Guardian in front of him. He had no idea how he had moved that quickly. He tried to push past the man standing in front of him but found it impossible to get by. Every time he moved forward the Guardian would push him back with a single hand. Alex grew more and more irritated and more convinced that he was on the right track with each failed attempt.

He shook his left hand and clenched and unclenched his fist. The vibration from his ring was growing stronger and he really wanted to hit this guy. He was going to find Liz and no one, not even this ancient guardian, was going to stop him. He clenched his fist once more, but this time it didn't unclench so easily. He nodded to himself and let go. He was surprised when his left hook connected with the Guardian's jaw. He had expected it to have no effect on the guy if he was able to make contact. It wouldn't have either if Alex had used his right and instead of his left.

"Ho-oly shit." Alex breathed out as he looked at the damage he had caused to the guy's face. The Guardian's once flawless square jaw now had a third degree burn where Alex's ring had made contact with his skin. The Guardian let out an animalistic growl and covered his face with his hand. Alex took advantage of this opening and attacked again. He knocked the staff out of the Guardian's hand and then hit him with a right hook to the rib cage. It didn't do much more than distract him as Alex came back with a left hook to his other side. His ring burned through the Guardian's robe and straight into his side. The Guardian reeled back, yelling in pain. Alex hit him again through the hole he had created in his robe. The Guardian fell to his knees and yelled out again. Alex punched him across the face once more, leaving a red streak deep across his cheek.

The Guardian, weakened by the power of Alex's ring, couldn't pick himself up off the floor. Alex kicked him hard in the rib cage and the Guardian fell over, bracing himself on his hands. As he fell forward, Alex kicked him in the face, sending him reeling back. When the Guardian fell backwards onto the floor Alex dropped to one knee beside him and raised his left hand high above him. He growled as he brought his fist down onto the Guardian's face, burning a hole into his skull.

He stood up and shook his hand trying to shake off the pain he felt from hitting him and trying to shake off what he had just done. He spared one more glance to the man lying motionless on the ground before grabbing his flashlight and his bag from where they had fallen. He took off down the tunnel, the light from his flashlight bouncing in rhythm with his

feet and his ring glowing with a bright blue hue.

Chapter 29

Liz stared at the Guardian standing in her way. She had expected to run into some sort of obstacle on her path, but the man standing in front of her is not what she had in mind. He looked to be much more than an ordinary person she thought as she approached with caution.

"I'm assuming you won't simply let me pass. What is it going to take for me to get by and be on my way?" She stood with her hands on her hips, staring into his dark eyes and waiting for an answer. When none came, she took a testing step forward. The Guardian shifted into a defensive stance, trying to push her back without actually touching her. She took one more step towards him and he held up his staff as if to warn her that he would strike her if she dared to move any closer. He still never made a sound. The fact that he hadn't said anything and stood there quietly staring at here made Liz shift uncomfortably from one foot to the other.

She considered her options. She was fairly certain she couldn't beat him in a straight fight. He would probably wipe the floor with her and then laugh about it later. She had to approach this very carefully or everything would be for not. Subconsciously she began to play with the ring that hung from the long chain around her neck. She still hadn't taken her eyes

off of the Guardian's face. She was hoping if she
looked him in the eyes, he would see she
wouldn't be intimidated by him. Whether it was
working or not, she had no idea. His expression
had been unchanged since she walked up. Now
she noticed, while his expression was the same,
his eyes were very carefully following the
movement of her ring. As she moved it back
and forth along the chain, his eyes moved back
and forth as well.

"Interesting...." She realized that the
rings her great grandmother had given her
might be more powerful than she had known.
She slipped the chain over her head and held it
in her hand. She let the ring dangle down and
began to swing it around casually; all the while

never taking her eyes off the Guardian. His eyes
continued to follow the ring's every move. She
took another step toward him and he flinched
just slightly. If she hadn't been watching him so
intently, she would have missed it. But, it was
there and she knew now what she had to do.
She began to spin the chain around in circles in
front of her and take slow calculated steps
toward him.

He took a small step backward with
each step she took forward, until he had backed
up against the stone wall behind him. He was
still watching her ring swing around on the
chain. He again held his staff up as if to defend
himself. She took another step closer, and he
struck out with it making contact with her

shoulder. She let out a pain filled yell and protectively covered the spot he had hit. She swung out with the chain and the ring made contact with his face. It left a deep red burning welt down his cheek, now it was his turn to vocalize his pain. Liz took half step back; she stood there looking at what she had done to his face, stunned that her simple gold band had done so much damage.

The Guardian shook his head to shake off the pain. He took a step away from the wall, his dark eyes boring into her. He adjusted his robe and raised his staff. Liz swallowed hard, this was about to get ugly and it was either going to be him or her. She adjusted her grip on the chain and crouched down slightly; waiting for him to make the first move. They stared at

each other for the longest time, each one

waiting for the other to move first. She shifted

her feet just a little bit and that was all it took

for him to come at her. She ducked his staff,

kicking her leg out and knocked his feet out

from under him. He fell, but only for a moment

and then he sprang back to his feet. He came at

her again, swinging the staff over his head.

Again, she ducked his attack but was

unprepared for him to come down right away.

He made contact with her head. She reeled

backward holding her head with her hand. Now

she was truly pissed off.

She wrapped the chain around her hand

making sure it was tight enough to keep the

ring on top. She waited for him to come at her
again; this time when she ducked his staff she
came back up with a fist to his side. Her ring
burned through his robe and into his side. He
jumped back, dropping his staff and holding his
rib cage. She kicked his staff out of reach and
looked at him with haughty eyes. This was going
to end now; it had to. The burns had weakened
him and she knew it. She didn't wait this time,
she went after him. He ducked her first swing,
but didn't account for her knee that came up
into his groin. He may have been an ancient
guardian, but he was still a man and the
connection dropped him to his knees. She took
that opportunity to come down hard on his

head with her chain wrapped hand. The ring burned into his skull and he fell to the ground.

Liz ran to the corner and quickly bent over in time to empty the contents of her stomach onto the dirt. She stood up and wiped her mouth and looked at the man lying in the middle of the round room. She didn't stay long though. She picked up her bag and flashlight and ran out of the room down the tunnel.

Chapter 30

Bob stood in the middle of the room and watched the events unfold. He couldn't take his eyes off the flickering images. He watched as Alex attacked the strange man. He flinched as his ring burned the man's face.

The only thing that was able to force him to look away from Alex's fight was Liz confronting the same man as Alex in what seemed like the same room. Bob felt his brain working over time trying to figure how that was even possible. His eyes darted back and forth following his thoughts.

"That's it! Oh, that's brilliant! That's bloody brilliant! It's a parallel universe!" Even as his logical side screamed that he was crazy,

deep down he had always believed there was

more to this world than anyone knew and was

as excited as a kid on Christmas. He had waited

his whole life for something like this.

Unfortunately one of his best friends was still

stuck in that parallel universe; even so, he

couldn't help but grin from ear to ear.

His grin quickly faded as he turned his

attention back to the images in front of him. He

was just in time to see Alex come down on the

strange man and burn a hole into his skull with

his ring. At the same time Liz also came down

hard on the man in her world, using her ring to

burn into his skull as well. He winced and

watched as Alex shook it off, grabbed his stuff

and took off down the tunnel. He looked away

when Liz threw up in the corner.

As Liz took off down the tunnel herself

both images faded to darkness. Bob slowly

backed up until he hit the wall behind him. He

slid down finding a ledge with his backside. He

set his pack on the ground and just sat there.

He couldn't wrap his head around what he had

just seen. It was easier for him to believe that

Alex had done what he did. But, he had never

thought Liz capable of something like that. He

swallowed hard to force down what was trying

to come up from his own stomach.

In that moment the reality of the

situation hit Bob. Up to this point he had seen

the whole thing as an adventure, maybe even a game. But sitting there, watching his friends defend themselves he realized that they could...die. Hell, he could die. He hadn't really let himself think of this as a life or death situation. He had just assumed that they would find Liz and everything would be fine. Now he was wondering what would happen if they never found her. He shook his head to clear away those thoughts, that wasn't an option. They would find her; they had to..

"Hang on, guys." He said to the flickering images in front of him. They were both mostly black, but occasionally he could just barely see Alex and Liz running through the tunnels, their rings glowing bright and the light

217

from their flashlights bouncing ahead of them.
He stood up and looked around the room he
was in. He still could not figure out where the
images on the wall in front of him were coming
from.

There had to be some connection
between the images he was seeing and a way
he could help them. He growled, he hated being
in situations where he felt helpless. He placed a
hand over his ribs and took a deep breath,
wincing the whole time. He kept his hand there
and began to walk around the room. He wasn't
sure what he was looking for, but he had a
feeling he would find it in there somewhere.

Chapter 31

As Alex ran through the tunnels, memories and images from his life played through his mind. They didn't seem to be in any particular order and he had no control over them. Images of his life with Liz would flash behind his eyes and the next instant childhood memories he had worked hard to forget would flash by.

Images from his wedding day rushed through his head; Alex smiled. He saw Liz walking toward him in a long white sundress. They were married just as summer was fading into fall and the leaves were just starting to shed their bright green coats for the red, orange

219

and yellow of autumn. She walked through the
field toward him and paused as she neared.
They locked eyes and smiled at each other. He
held out his hand to her and they stood
together in front of God, the minister, their
closest friends and her family.

The next memory hit him so hard and
fast that he had to stop running and brace
himself against the wall of the tunnel. He shook
his head trying to shake free of the memory.
But, it was not letting go of him and it played
through his head slower than the rest. The one
memory he had worked so hard to forget was
playing through his head in real time. It was like
he was there, back in that cramped and dirty
trailer. It was the day before he turned sixteen.

His aunt had come home drunk, again, and she wasn't alone. Her "boyfriend" was with her. Alex had pretended to be asleep on his bed in the corner of the front room when they came in. He hadn't seen his aunt in days and was too tired for a confrontation. He wasn't going to be that lucky though; his aunt's friend came over to where he was laying on nothing more than a thin mattress on the floor and kicked him hard in his side.

"Hey, you fucking free loader...Get up!" Another kick. "I said get up you pussy!"

Alex pushed himself up, being careful to not let the jackass see him wince. He stood up to his full height, six feet even at fifteen. He faced the guy square and looked straight into his eyes not saying a word. He'd had it this time. For years he had listened to this asshole verbally and physically abuse his aunt and even felt the sting himself. He had never been able to do anything about it before because he was too small. This time was different. It had been nearly six months since his aunt had brought the abusive low life home and Alex was ready now. He knew what he had to do. He let his anger run through his body and clenched and unclenched his fists to release just enough so he didn't explode.

"What are you looking at you piece of shit?" The guy spat the words into Alex's face and pushed him backward. Alex took half a step back and stood his ground. This seemed to anger the guy even more and he finally did what Alex was waiting for. He rushed him. There was very little room to move around in that little trailer. But, Alex had been secretly training over the past twelve months and he was prepared. He used the momentum and the guy's immense weight against him and threw him to the floor. He kicked him hard in his side when the guy got to his knees to try to stand up. When that didn't knock him back down, Alex came down with both fists onto his back. This sent him sprawling on the floor and Alex jumped onto him and started hitting him over and over again.

"Alex, STOP IT! Just STOP IT!" His aunt screamed while trying to pull him off. With one last punch he wiped his mouth and stood up. He stood there for a moment watching his aunt cry and check over the wounds on the jerk off she kept going back to. She looked up at Alex with her mascara stained faced and he knew what was coming. He shook his head, put his shoes on and grabbed the bag he had already packed. He was planning on leaving in the morning anyway, but now was as good of time as any.

"Don't worry, I'm gone." He said as he walked out the door. He never saw or heard from his aunt again and never knew how much she had actually remembered the next morning. That was the moment that had defined most of his adult life. He had suffered years of abuse at that man's hands and had finally stood up for himself and his aunt only to lose the only family he had left because of it. He had chosen to forget about his past because he didn't believe that love and family loyalty really existed.

When the memory stopped, it was as if Alex was literally being sucked out of the past and he was left breathing hard. His head ached from the strength of a memory that had been stored so far back in his mind. He had never even told Liz about his aunt or that night. He wiped the sweat off of his face with his sleeve and tried to stand up straight. The effects seemed to be wearing off quickly and he was ready to continue on once again.

As he turned to continue on, he was suddenly face to face with another Guardian. He sighed and dropped his head. *Really?* He thought. He was so tired and worn out, and he didn't have time for this. The Guardian took his stance like he was going to stop Alex from continuing. Alex stretched his neck from side to side and was greeted with a welcome pop. He rolled his head up and looked at the Guardian. He really wasn't in the mood for this. He shook his head and struck out with his left hand. His fist made contact with the Guardian's chest. He barely had time to realize that contact was made before his fist had burned straight through the Guardian's chest and he fell backward onto the ground. Alex grabbed a rag out of his pocket and wiped his hand off before

continuing on his way.

Chapter 32

Liz ran for as long as she could and then slowed her pace to a quick, clipped walked. She breathed deep through her nose and out through her mouth trying to slow her heart rate. Her flashlight began to flicker so she turned it off, her eyes slowly adjusting to the dim glow of her ring that hung on the chain from her hand. She looked around as she walked. She was hoping for any sign of change in the walls. She felt like she had walked in a straight line for an eternity. The silence of the underground tunnel was deafening. The only sound she could hear was the beating of her own heart, it seemed to fill her ears and echo through her head.

Liz squinted into the distance. She wasn't sure she was really seeing what she thought she was. She thought there was a bend in the wall ahead of her. She was so focused on that possible change, she barely registered the strange clicking sound that had joined with the rhythm of her own hear beat. *Click-click...click-click...click-click.* Liz turned her head from side to side, trying to place where the clicking was coming from. She took the chance and turned her flashlight back on just hoping the batteries would hold out. *Click-click...click-click...click-click.*

She shone her light around deliberately, looking in all the corners in front of her. *Click-click...click-click...* Liz gradually turned around

and shone her flashlight behind her. *Click click.*
She gasped and found herself screaming when
she saw it. Slowly emerging from the darkness
she saw a long, hairy leg and then another.
Then she found herself staring into the multiple
eyes of an enormous black spider that was
towering over her. She took two cautious steps
backwards, her breath catching in her throat.
She couldn't look away from her reflection in
the glassy black eyes in front of her.

Liz took another step backward and
then another. Before she knew it, she felt her
back hit the cool wall of the tunnel. She still
couldn't take her eyes off of the monster in
front of her. *Click-click...Click-click.* She let out
the breath she hadn't even realized she was

holding. When she breathed in again she smelled an odd odor she could only assume was coming from the spider standing in front of her. She couldn't quite place what the smell was; it was a strange combination of a musky body odor and bad breath. *Click-click...click-click.*

Liz took the chance and glanced away. She looked from one side to the other not daring to lift her head from the wall behind her. She was afraid that any sudden movement could bring on an attack that she wasn't sure she could counter or respond to. *Come on, Liz. You can do this. Think..just breath and think.* Liz racked her brain trying desperately to figure out how fight this gigantic spider she never even imagined could exist. *Click-click.* She stopped moving completely when she noticed

movement out of the corner of her eye. She

slowly turned her head, her hair rubbing against

the damp dirt and stone behind her. When she

was once again facing the spider she noticed

that the last of its legs had just stopped moving

and it was standing significantly closer to her

than it was before.

Click-click...Click-click...Click-click. She

felt tears sting her eyes and tried to blink them

back. She let out her breath, her chin quivering

with fear. Liz once again slowly turned her

head, keeping one eye on the spider while still

trying to find some sort of weapon in this dark,

abandoned mineshaft. She could feel the

spider's breath on her face, which she found

232

strange because she wasn't really sure how

spiders breathed. It was then that she spotted

it. She couldn't believe she had missed it

before, it was right there in front of her! Now

she just had to figure out how to reach it. She

glanced up the wall and at the spider and

back...how was she going to reach the torch and

how was she going to get it lit? *Click-*

Click...Click-Click...Click-Click.

Chapter 33

Bob was searching around the room in the back of the cave when he saw movement out of the corner of his eye. He turned around and looked at the images on the wall that were once again flashing. Alex seemed to be suffering, but not from anything Bob could see. He furrowed his brow wondering what could be so bad that Alex was leaning against the wall as if his life depended on it. He shook his head and glanced over at the images of Liz.

Bob gasped, "Holy shit!" He unconsciously took a step back from the image in front of him. He couldn't believe what he was looking at. He had never seen a spider that big in his life! It had Liz backed up against the wall and he could tell she was trying not to panic. She was slowly turning her head from side to side; he was guessing she was looking for some sort of weapon. Bob had no idea how she was going to get out that. He didn't want to look away even for a second, but he forced himself to tear his eyes away. He knew there was nothing he could do for her. However, he still felt like there was an answer here somewhere.

He walked back over to the other side of the room where he had been searching. There was something off about that wall. He couldn't put his finger on it, but he knew there was something not right. He ran his hand up and down the section of the wall that didn't look right, he was hoping to feel a burst of air or

a seam; anything to prove his instincts were

right. Just as he was about to give up and move

on, he took a small step to the right and felt

something give under his foot. He looked down

and noticed what he had thought was a small

rock was actually a depression switch. He heard

rock slowly sliding against rock and looked up.

In the exact place he had been examining, a

door slid open.

He glanced over his shoulder giving the

flashing images one more look. It hurt him to

see his friends suffering so much. He took a

deep breath and walked through the door,

hoping to find a way to help them out. He

wasn't sure what he expected to find in the

hidden room, but what he saw was definitely not it.

"Bloody Hell." He whispered. He stood just inside the door, his mouth hanging open in shock. He was looking at some sort of control room. The controls were unlike anything he had seen before. Each control seemed to be made from crystals and precious gems. They were all glowing and it was impossible to tell exactly what they controlled. If he was ever going to find a way to help Alex and Liz, this was where it was going to be. Just as he took another step into the room he heard a noise behind him. He turned to look and his eyes widened.

"NOooo!" He screamed and the whole world went black.

Chapter 34

Click-click…Click-click. Liz slid slowly

down the wall toward the torch. She moved

inch by inch, never taking her eyes off of the

monster in front of her. She had to time

everything just right. She had to pull it off, she

could beat this thing. She knew she was only

going to get one shot at it though. Finally, she

reached the spot where the torch was just

above her head on the wall. She cautiously

tilted her head back to judge the distance of the

reach to the torch handle. She was guessing,

but it looked to be just within arm's reach.

Now came the tricky part; lighting the

torch. She had no matches and no lighter. Liz

knew she was going to have to tap into a part of

her powers, a part of herself that had been

dormant for a long time. She had utilized a

small part of her powers over the years; the

knowing part. The rest, though, she had refused

to use since she was a teenager. Her

grandmother had made sure she was well

prepared and could control them. But, after she

had gone back home to her parents, Liz had

repressed the abilities in order to be accepted

by them. She threw herself into her school; that

dedication had not only gotten her into one of

the best Ivy League colleges in the country, but

had given Liz her parent's acceptance as well.

Now in this dark tunnel, she would have

to tap into that part of herself. Liz closed her

eyes and took a deep breath. *Mimi, give me the strength. Flow through me and help me.* Liz concentrated all her energy on the torch above her. *Click-click...Click-click...Click-click...Click-click.* She could tell the spider was becoming more and more agitated, but she forced herself to tune out its constant clicking and focus on lighting the torch. She tilted her head from side to side, stretching her neck muscles.

Liz took another deep breath and slowly let it out. *Come on, Liz. You can do this. This is who you are...This is your destiny. You're running out of time, now concentrate and do it! NOW, dammit!* She wanted to shut her inner voice up, but knew it was right. She visualized the torch bursting into flames and mentally

241

pushed her energy up towards it. She thought she felt something, but was sure it was all in her head and that she had failed. She was going to die here and never make it back to Alex. Defeated she slowly opened her eyes and looked at the spider.

Click...Click...Click. Liz paused and furrowed her brow. Something was different. The spider's clicking had changed; it was slower now and less confident. If it was possible, Liz could swear she saw fear in the monster's many eyes. She chanced looking up and saw that the torch was lit; the flames were reaching high up toward the ceiling and putting off an unusual amount of heat. Liz's face broke out into a grin that went from ear to ear. She couldn't believe it had worked!

"Thank you, Mimi! Thank you!" She whispered. *Click-Click, Click-click, click-click.* Liz turned back to the spider as the clicking grew faster and more intense. She knew it was now or never. The spider seemed to crouch just slightly, getting ready for the attack. Liz could feel her heart beating faster in her chest and her hands began to shake just a little bit from the adrenaline that was pumping though her body. She reached her arm up just above her shoulder, waiting for the right moment.

The next few seconds were a blur. The spider attacked, Liz grabbed for the torch and pushed it into the monster's eyes. The spider let

out the most horrific scream Liz had ever heard.

She had to force herself to keep the fire in its

face until the screaming stopped. Once it had,

she dropped the torch on the floor and stood

there staring at the body of the monster she

had defeated. She ran her hands down her face

and wiped the sweat on her pants. Liz let out

the breath she had been holding and slowly

turned her back to the spider lying motionless

on the floor. She bent down and picked up her

flashlight, now working fine, and her bag. Liz

gave one last glance over her shoulder as she

continued into the mine and toward her

destiny... and her love.

Chapter 35

Alex was still trying to wipe the blood

off of his hand when he found himself in a large

open room deep inside the mine. He hadn't

been in many mines in his day, but even he was

pretty sure this was not normal. It seemed to be

some sort of altar room. He stood in the

doorway trying to take it all in.

"What the hell?" he said under his

breath. It was like nothing he had ever seen

before. Ancient statues he couldn't quite place

carved out of granite stood floor to ceiling and

circled the room. They seemed to loom over

him, giving him a feeling of dread in the pit of

his stomach. In the center of the room was a

stone alter with intricate and detailed carvings on all sides. From a distance they seemed to depict a battle of some sort.

He took a couple of cautious steps into the room, making sure the floor wasn't booby trapped or something crazy like that. When he decided it probably wasn't and he didn't have time to be sure anyway, he crossed to the center of the room to the altar. On the top of it, he noticed writing engraved. It was the same kind of lettering that was engraved on his ring. He also noticed that as he stood there next to it, his ring was beginning to heat up.

He kneeled down to examine the carvings surrounding the altar. As he ran his fingers over the incredible details he noticed that it wasn't a battle it was showing, but a ceremony. From what he could tell, the ceremony was to curse an entire society. He couldn't imagine what would make someone want to do something like that. He knew the world was far from perfect, more so than a lot of people did, but to curse a whole society and sacrifice thousands of innocent people to punish a few truly evil ones was beyond him.

"Oh my god..." he breathed as he followed the pictures around the altar. He couldn't be sure if he was translating the pictures correctly. He still was unable to place what time frame or even exactly what people made all this. It seemed to be a culture more ancient than he had ever come across before.

He wasn't sure anyone had any knowledge of

these people. If he was reading it right, anyone

who was caught up in the curse was

transported to an alternate plain. There they

were forced into a time loop where everyone

was doomed to relieve their greatest sins over

and over again for all eternity. That meant that

the innocent people caught in the curses pull

had to evolve into something evil simply to

survive or to just let the others take them and

end their suffering. That's when it all hit him.

"DAMMIT, LIZ!" He yelled into the

darkness. "You knew! The whole time you were

insisting we come here for that dig. You knew!

You knew about the curse and you knew when

it would come full circle to strike again. You knew and you didn't tell me. You didn't tell me because you also knew that I would try to stop you. Dammit, Liz, dammit!"

Alex knew he could be mad at Liz later. Right now he had to figure out how to get her out and soon. If he didn't figure something out fast, he could lose her forever. She wasn't really gone, not yet, he could feel it. He shook his left hand. Suddenly his ring felt like it was going to burn straight through his finger. He looked down and saw that the subtle blue glow had turned red.

It was then that he noticed there was a strange spot on top of the altar. It was a small round engraving that could only fit one thing.

Alex hesitated though. It did seem as though it

was missing something. He had to be right

about this. He was only going to get one shot at

saving Liz. He closed his eyes and slowly slid his

ring off of his finger. He brought it to his lips

and felt the burn of the hot metal as he kissed it

and then carefully placed it in the circle on the

altar. All at once the entire room was filled with

a bright white light. Alex shaded his eyes and

took a step back from the altar.

"Alex? Alex, are you there?"

Alex felt tears burn in his eyes at the

sound of that familiar voice. It was the voice

that had changed his life and lit up his world. It

was the voice that had haunted his dreams and ran through his head for all these long months. He squinted, trying to see through the blinding light. He frantically looked around the room. Where could she be? He could feel her and he could hear her, but he couldn't see her.

"Liz! Liz, honey, where are you? I'm here!"

Just then he felt himself thrown backward as a cold explosion vibrated through the room. His head hit hard against the foot of one of the statues. He had time to feel a single tear run down his cheek and one thought to run through his head; he had failed. Then everything went black. He could feel himself being pulled back toward reality, but he didn't

want to go. Liz was gone, lost to the curse

forever and it was all his fault. He had failed and

it had cost him the love of his life and most

likely his best friend as well. What had

happened to Bob?

He fought as hard as he could to stay in

that empty void of darkness for as long as he

could. It was the sudden slap of a tiny hand on

his face that finally brought him back. He knew

that hand! Alex slowly opened his eyes and

blinked a few times to clear his vision. When he

could see clearly again he was staring into the

clearest, bluest eyes he had ever seen. The eyes

he had lost himself in every time he looked into

them over the years. He tried to sit up, but his

head felt heavy and he laid back down never

taking his eyes off hers.

He knew in that moment that he had

succeeded after all. He lay there for as long as

he could take it. Her face broke out into the

smile that had made him fall in love with her he

sat straight up, pain be damned. He grabbed

her in his arms and held her tight. He pulled

away just slightly, brushing the hair from her

face. He smiled back at her and closed the

distance between them. Their first kiss had

been incredible, but this one topped even that

one.

"I thought I had lost you. I couldn't

breathe I missed you so much, Liz. God, I love

you." Liz looked down at her ring and ran her

thumb over the engraving.

"True love will find its strength from

within." Alex wanted to be mad at her for

keeping all this from him. But, all he cared

about was the fact that she was here. He smiled

and pulled her close once again. He knew that

from this moment, he would never let her go

again.

Epilogue

Alex pushed open the screen door smiling at the familiar squeak. As he stepped out onto the porch, he paused for a moment and breathed in the cool mountain air. The beer bottles clinked together in his hand has he walked across the well-worn porch. He grinned as he stole a kiss from Liz as she took one of the bottles from him.

"Get a bloody room will you?" Bob said jokingly as he accepted one of the two remaining bottles from Alex. It had been three months since they had returned from California and his wounds had almost healed. Alex and Liz had insisted he stay with them during his recovery and as much as he had pretended to refuse, he was grateful to them and all their help.

"Pipe down, you! It's not my fault you tripped and got off easy with this whole thing!"

"You call this easy?" Bob said showcasing his still healing injuries. "Also, I didn't bloody trip... I was attacked." He paused and rubbed the back of his head. "I just don't happen to remember what it was that attacked me."

"Whatever you say, Buddy." Alex joked as he clapped Bob on the shoulder.

They all shared a laugh as Alex took the empty chair on the other side of Liz. He casually rested his feet on the porch rail in front of him

and took Liz's hand in his. He couldn't seem to

keep the smile from spreading across his face.

He'd had that problem a lot over the past few

months. But, he didn't mind. He was one lucky

guy. He glanced over at Bob, they thought

they'd lost him. Now he was sitting there giving

Liz a hard time like he always did. Alex raised his

bottle to him and nodded his head. Bob raised

his bottle in return, and unspoken cheers

between two friends who were closer than

brothers. Alex squeezed Liz's hand and felt his

ring rub against the cold bottle in his left hand.

He was afraid he'd lost it when he broke the

curse. Liz thought to check the altar, now

cracked down the center, before they left the

mine though. Sure enough his ring was still sitting in the circle engraving on top. She had slid it back on his finger and he hadn't taken it off again since.

"Well, mates, I supposed there is one pressing matter we must attend to…" Alex and Liz looked at each other, both wondering what Bob could possibly be referring to. They looked over at him waiting impatiently. Alex gestured for him to hurry up and spit it out. Bob shrugged and as he lifted the bottle to his lips asked, "What's next?"

The Curse

Mandy Baker has been a Coast Guard wife for more than a decade. She currently lives in Connecticut with her husband and their cat, a spoiled Calico named Missy. She is in the process of earning her Bachelor's Degree in English. When she isn't writing, she can usually be found behind her camera taking pictures of her life and the world around her.

The Curse